The Three of Them

Zeke Jarvis

ISBN: 978-1-62420-489-0

Credits
Cover Artist: Designs by Ms G
Editor: Deborah C. Day

Dedication

For Cas

The Three of Them

Without hearing a word, Harper knew that the boys were laughing and she knew that they were laughing at her. She didn't need to use psychic powers to get the main points of what they were saying. Harper could have picked up the specifics if she wanted, but, honestly, she didn't want to know. Maybe Steven was pretending to ask Mike if she was walking funny or trying to twerk. Maybe Mike was saying he had something that could make her walk straight for once.

Harper had heard those jokes (or ones just like them) many times before, both out loud and in the boys' heads. The first few times she'd heard them she tried to read the boys' thoughts. She wanted to see what they were thinking, what made them say such gross things. Sometimes the boys would be thinking disgusting things, thinking about her body or some other poor girl's. Sometimes it would be about impressing the other boys. Either way, it was never something that she was glad to find out, so she'd just stopped trying.

Today, Harper took a quick glance and she thought she saw something in Mike's face. Something weird. She decided to come back to it later, when he was alone and probably not thinking about her. For now, she just kept walking away from the two goons. As Harper's mother would say, even if boys were jerks, she still had to make it to first period on time. At least math was just boring instead of being gross.

Harper got to her locker and set her backpack on the floor. She moved her backpack into her locker and pulled out her notebook while the rest of the students in the hall kept moving, bumping and jabbering with each other. Harper hated hallway traffic. It wasn't that it was dangerous. She hadn't actually been knocked over since elementary school, and she'd had years of physical therapy and adaptive PE since then. The problem with the hall traffic was that it was thoughtless. Like if you had an army of robots, but instead of being laser-shooting killing machines, they were just dumbasses who were programmed to only talk about clothes or football and who would just stare at you if you said "excuse me" to try to get them to move.

The first bell rang. Harper knew that she still had a little bit of time, but not so much that she could fool around. She finished getting her things and closed up her locker, pulling on the lock once to make sure that it had clicked. She slid into the hallway crush, sticking to the right side to avoid the people in a hurry.

Harper watched some of the hurriers weave in and out of traffic. There went Ella, probably in a hurry to get a jump start on some chemistry project or to meet with a teacher about starting some club. She would lean and speed up or slow down to avoid running into anyone. It was impressive. It made her seem like she could've been an athlete if she wanted. Harper watched her go until she ran into a herd of football players that were blocking her way. Ella was trying to find a gap when Harper hung a right to get to her classroom. She was halfway to the door when someone bumped into her. It didn't knock her all the way down, but she did have to steady herself against the wall.

It was some guy texting and walking. He didn't even turn around to say that he was sorry. Harper listened to him quickly. It was the usual mix of boring song lyrics, worry about girls and annoyance about how slow his phone was. Harper tuned back out. Sometimes she had trouble coordinating her reading and getting around without running into things. She could chalk that up to her CP most times if people asked, but it could still be annoying and embarrassing.

Harper made it into the room and to her desk with a few minutes to spare. As usual, Mr. Spade was writing equations on the board, his back to all the students. Harper had listened to his thoughts once or twice (as she had with pretty much all of her teachers and her principal). As far as she could tell, he had nearly a constant loop of second-guessing himself running through his head. He might be thinking that he shouldn't have had such a heavy meal for lunch, or he might be wondering if he shouldn't have ended a conversation with another teacher so quickly. Some days Harper felt bad for him, having to teach math (one of the most hated subjects) to a bunch of little jerks while doubting himself for a ton of different reasons.

Today, though, Harper didn't feel a whole lot of sympathy. Not that Mr. Spade was doing anything particularly annoying today (other than writing a bunch of sine and cosine problems on the board). There was just something bothering her today, she realized. Not just the boys, though they didn't help. There was something else. Like a weird energy in the school.

Harper tried to shake it off as she got out her pencil, calculator, and notebook. Mr. Spade finished writing one last equation. He put down his dry-erase marker, but he didn't turn around yet. He never did that until the bell rang. As Harper waited, she heard talking and laughing behind her.

Harper tried to ignore the laughing. She looked out of the classroom door. There was Ella, sprinting by the door. Harper wondered if she would make it to class on time. She also wondered if Ella might play by a different set of rules than she did. Harper had her own set of rules, in a sense. It was all laid out in her IEP, in those meetings she had to sit through where everyone explained how remarkable it was that she could do what other students could. But Ella's different rules were different than Harper's different rules. Ella could point to things. Harper could point to things, but they were different things, and that was what was frustrating. The bell rang. A new kind of frustrating started.

~ * ~

Krista jumped a little when she turned around. Who knows how long her mom had been standing behind her like a stalker? Krista hadn't noticed her mom blocking the light or smelling of too much perfume or anything like she did sometimes. Krista gave a smile and went towards the fridge, not taking her eyes off her mother. "Hey."

Her mom stopped rubbing her eye and nodded a little. "Homework done?"

"Mostly. I'll finish after a snack." Krista let the door slowly swing shut as she went back to the counter.

"Don't ruin your dinner."

Krista nodded. She opened the bread bag and took out two slices. Her mom just stood there, kind of watching. Krista dropped a knife into the peanut butter jar and started spreading it on the bread. "How was work?"

"Huh?" Her mom squinted just a little.

Krista decided not to press her luck. Instead, she finished spreading the peanut butter and licked the extra off the knife.

"Don't ruin your dinner," her mom said again.

Krista nodded and started to clean up. Her mom yawned and went back to her room, shuffling off in her sad and semi-creepy way. Another drag in an already strange day. Now it was both school and home where she had people sneaking up on her. She grabbed a paper towel and brought it and her sandwich back to her room.

When Krista got there, she closed the door and went to her bed. She guessed that her mom had laid down to watch TV and wouldn't bother her again for a while. Krista closed her eyes and took a bite. The world was almost fully shut out. She was almost able to enjoy her life for a few seconds. Just her and her generic peanut butter. Even that didn't last long as all the crap of the school day crept into her head.

Krista opened her eyes. Her door was still closed, thankfully. She reached over to her nightstand and grabbed her soda. It was warm by now, but at least it washed down the peanut butter. Krista replayed the day's events in her mind, thinking about whether or not she'd been careless when she'd turned invisible. It didn't seem like she'd been any more careless than usual. She'd waited until all the other girls were already in there, pretending that taking out her hearing aids slowed her down.

After turning invisible, she'd been very careful to walk without bumping into anyone. She'd showered in the corner, her back towards the walls, watching the other girls as she soaped up and rinsed off right away. The last things she needed was for someone to notice floating bubbles, but having some stuck-up blonde telling her how fat she was wasn't far behind on the list. So she waited a bit, making sure there was a clear shot for her to sneak out of the shower. It looked like she had one, but right before she made her way from the showers to the lockers, some girl tried to turn around and go back in for something. Krista was able to steady herself against a wall, but the girl slipped and fell. Right away, everyone broke into their predictable camps. About a third of the girls went to the girl who had slipped. They asked her what happened. Krista was able to sneak out while the girl tried to figure it out for herself without losing the other's attention.

Another third of the girls in class just shrugged it off and went on their way, brushing their hair or toweling off. The last group laughed quietly and started spinning their gossip before the poor girl even finished her story. It was sickening without being surprising.

Krista managed to grab a towel and go to the back of the locker room, where she dried off and let herself become visible again. She wrapped the towel around herself and went to her locker. While Krista was opening it, she could feel someone watching her. Her hearing aids were still out, so she could pretend that she was oblivious, but she could feel it.

Krista opened her locker, using the door like a shield. After she got her stuff out though, there was no more hiding. There was only Jenna. Jenna was the kind of mean that would wait patiently while her victim squirmed. Krista turned towards her and pretended to be surprised. "Jenna. Didn't see you there."

"I'm here," she said. Krista wanted to punch her in the face.

Jenna went on. "I didn't see you in the shower."

Krista tried very hard to keep a straight face. "Were you looking?"

Jenna gave an almost smile. "You're so funny," she said.

Krista just wanted to be done with Jenna, so she leaned forward a little and said, "Huh?" hoping that her deafness would be enough of a bother to keep her from asking any more questions.

It was hard to tell if Jenna knew that she was being lied to or not. Either way, she just nodded and said, "Well, I'll see you around."

It had been a sad mix of creepy and mildly annoying. Now, eating her sandwich, Krista wondered if Jenna was a sign that something was even worse than usual in the school or if it was just a coincidence that she and Harper were having off days. Of course, they'd have to look into it. Harper wouldn't let it go. That was probably for the best, but it was still a pain and Krista still had to finish her science homework. She took a last bite of her sandwich, slugged some soda, and opened her book.

~ * ~

James was finishing up his math homework when his mother came into his room. "How was your day, James?"

"Good."

James's mother stood by him quietly for a moment. "Anything exciting happen?"

James finished calculating a derivative and then tried to think. The comments from the football players would lead to concern from his mother and additional questions. Any interactions with either Krista or Harper could be interpreted as potential for romance, and that would also lead to more questions. The homecoming theme could be deemed exciting without putting focus on James. "This year's homecoming theme is superheroes."

"Cool," his mother said. "Are they doing dress-up days?"

"On Friday, we can wear some kind of costume, provided that it's appropriate."

"Well that'll be fun. Who are you going as?"

As a rule, James did not participate in school activities, and this one in particular seemed likely to result in teasing. "I haven't decided yet."

"Hmm," his mother said. "Well, there's still time to decide, right?"

James said, "Or to decide that a costume is not of interest."

His mother smiled. "I'm glad you're not letting it worry you."

James put down his pencil and closed his book, but decided he wouldn't look up at his mother. They stayed silent for a moment before she said, "Well, dinner should be ready pretty soon."

"Okay." James ran through what assignments he'd completed and what he had left. He'd finished English, math, chemistry and history. He could finish computer science after dinner, and all he had to do for American government was watch a video, though he wasn't entirely sure what the point of that was.

James's mother touched his shoulder and then left his room. James thought about the superhero figures he had received at age ten. He'd taken a talking Spiderman figure apart. He understood now that was an inappropriate way to demonstrate appreciation for the toy, but at the time being able to explore the system of wiring had been interesting. Much more interesting than pretending that the figure had its own thoughts and emotions.

Next, James wondered if part of Harper's interest in trying to keep the school and the people in it safe was simply a hero fantasy. He recognized that it was unlikely that Harper had received the same type of encouragement to like superheroes that he had as a child, but maybe she was impacted by the social pressures that Mrs. Peterson kept talking about in regards to issues of race, gender, and social class.

James decided against asking Harper directly. She often did not take such questions well, and she seemed particularly concerned in school today. James didn't understand what she meant when she told him and Krista that something was "off" in the school (and James was pleased to see that Krista expressed skepticism as well), but he recognized that she would likely be combative for at least the next day, if not the rest of the week because of his follow-up questions. That kind of reaction was not out of the ordinary. The problem was how to prove or disprove things. How can a person measure whether or not the school is "creepier"? Imprecision in language always led to imprecision in measurement.

And yet, maybe there was some way to track things like the level of aggression throughout the school. Or if there was a way to track visits to the nurse's office, suggesting that people were seeking out comfort or feeling physical discomfort because of emotional problems. These might be able to challenge (or possibly justify) Harper's theory that something was wrong. But what to focus on first? And how could he take a baseline or control measurement? If things had already become "creepy," then it was too late to establish what the normal rates were.

James closed his eyes. He pictured the drawer in his desk just to the left of his knee. He focused not on the handle, as he had the first time he'd tested his ability, but instead upon the rollers on each side of the drawer's tracks. He focused on making them rotate, slowly pushing the drawer open. When James opened his eyes, the task had been completed. At least his powers still worked.

~ * ~

"I can't just turn invisible and walk through walls," Krista said. "I have to get into somewhere first and I have to turn invisible off-camera in case someone sees the tape."

"Okay," Harper said.

"In addition to those logistical issues, there's no guarantee that either the teachers or principal would know any more than we do." He took a bite of his pizza and looked away.

"Okay," Harper said again. She crossed her arms.

James pushed the food in his mouth to one cheek and said, "In fact, Harper, given your talents, you likely are more aware of the problem."

Krista raised her eyebrows and pointed at James, nodding. Harper just sighed. "Fine," she said. "I guess all we can do is sit back and wait for the murders to start."

"Oh God," Krista said. She looked away, watching one of the popular tables. There was Jenna, but instead of talking to her friends about either boys or make-up, Jenna was just quietly eating her lunch and watching Krista. Krista smiled and waved. Before Jenna had a chance to wave back, Krista turned towards Harper. "Don't look over now, but is Jenna up to something?"

Harper looked down at her sandwich. She was quiet for a moment, then said, "This is weird."

She was quiet again, so Krista said, "What is it?"

"Her thoughts are like, I don't know. They feel different than how most people think."

James cleared his throat. "In all fairness, you might say that about me."

"No," Harper said, "This is different. It's like trying to listen to a different language."

"I knew it," Krista said. "She's a damn demon."

"Don't be an ass," Harper said.

Krista shrugged and put a Dorito in her mouth. "You're the one who thought something weird or creepy was going on."

Harper looked over at Jenna, briefly, then back at the table. There was a blankness to Jenna's face that creeped Harper out. The usual snobbery and low level of hatred wasn't there. It was like the feeling you get when you're alone with a portrait and the eyes seem to follow you wherever you go.

"Do you think she's the cause or the effect?" James asked.

"What?" Harper asked.

"Of the so-called creepiness," he said. "Is she causing it or is she the product of it?"

Harper hadn't even considered the question, but leave it to James to think of it. "I can't say yet. I've never felt something like this before."

Krista said, "Who would've thought someday we'd actually be interested in what was going through Jenna's mind?"

"If it's still hers," James said.

Krista dumped the rest of the Doritos from the bag into her right hand. "Well, it's not like she was going to use it."

Harper crumpled up an empty baggie. "Don't try to laugh it off too much. We don't know what this could be the start of."

James said, "Maybe you should try some of the others at Jenna's table to see if they're also abnormal." He then finished his pizza.

"Abnormal?" Harper asked.

Harper sighed and focused. Krista wiped her hands on a napkin, and James drank his water. After a minute or two, Harper said, "The rest are normal. Jenny is worried that her mom will find her pot stash, Tina is sad she's not thinner, and Ethan is thinking about how to hide the fact that he's gay?"

"Ethan's gay?" James said.

"God, James," Krista said. "Well, at least we know that it's just Jenna."

Harper took a bite of her sandwich. She wasn't entirely sure how she felt about it being just Jenna. "Even if that's true, what do we do?"

James separated his trash from his recyclables. "Continued observation is the next step. We need to know what she can do."

Krista said, "Crap, that's a scary thought. Who knows how much power she might have?"

"And how do we find out?" Harper asked. "Obviously we can't ask her."

James put his recyclables back in his lunch bag. "It would be a mistake to confront her directly at this point."

Krista looked over at Jenna again. She was still looking and with the same expression on her face. "Let's figure it out *before* she eats my face or something."

James said, "Your muscle would be more satisfying to eat than your skin."

"Might depend on how she's cooked, James," Harper said.

"Knock it off," Krista said. "She's not staring at either of you."

"All right," Harper said. "We'll all brainstorm tonight and compare ideas tomorrow."

~ * ~

Again in the locker room, Jenna was waiting for Krista. Krista hadn't turned herself invisible this time, and Jenna was waiting. "What were you and the other two talking about at lunch today?"

Krista tried to keep her face calm, not letting her lip twitch like it did sometimes. "We were just talking about you."

Jenna laughed. "Must've been exciting." It was the kind of thing that typical Jenna might say, pretending to be joking.

"We felt like there's something different about you." Krista watched Jenna's face carefully, trying to see if she blushed, if her eyes narrowed. Nothing. "Doing your hair differently, maybe?"

Jenna ran her fingers through her hair. "Not really. I mean, I've started using a new conditioner, but I don't think it shows."

Krista nodded. "Either way, you look nice." It was hard to stay calm and watch Jenna while being naked under a ratty school towel.

"Thanks," Jenna said. "Maybe you should try a new conditioner sometime."

That definitely sounded like typical Jenna. Krista tried not to let her own cheeks turn red. "Maybe you could recommend your brand, unless it's a secret."

Jenna laughed a little. "Yeah, I have all kinds of secrets."

Krista couldn't help it. This time, she shivered. She turned away.

Jenna said something, though Krista wasn't entirely sure what. When Krista got to her locker, she felt dizzy. She thought about closing her eyes, but she worried that it might just make things worse. Instead, Krista sat down on the bench and just stared ahead. Eventually, her head stabilized. She stood up slowly and started to put the combination into her lock when she saw a shadow cast over her locker. Of course, it was Jenna.

Jenna looked down at Krista. "Feel better soon."

Krista watched Jenna walk off. For the first time in a long time, Krista wondered if the school had more than just three students hiding powers.

~ * ~

James tried hard not to hate the football players. They knew how to make fun of him without getting caught. That was their special ability. Case in point: Derrick, who James believed was a defensive back, was making a slack face behind James. Derrick must have assumed that James couldn't see this. Or maybe he just didn't care. But James was looking at the window. In the reflection, he could see Derrick as well as two other football players, laughing. This frustrated James in two ways. First, he felt the sense of isolation that any person feels from being the object of ridicule. Second, there was the frustration of knowing that he was not supposed to use his powers to retaliate. If he wanted to, for instance, James could wait until class was over, and then focus on Derrick's pant's waist, pulling his pants down in front of everyone and then pulling the pants backwards so that they would trip Derrick, leaving him face down on the floor.

Despite the fact that James was fully capable of these acts, he was forbidden from doing them for a number of reasons. The two most compelling reasons were that there would be some kind of investigation or attention that could result in either his powers being discovered or another student being wrongfully blamed, and that it was morally questionable to exert his power over someone else for his own pleasure (even though James could think of dozens of examples of people performing similar actions in school on a daily basis).

James wondered if there was a way to have Jenna display her

powers on Derrick and/or the other football players. This would be more than just punishing the football players. It would more precisely be a careful selection of a test subject in order to gain information that would help the entire school. Still, James didn't think that Harper would allow it, though perhaps he would be able to convince Krista to support it.

James focused on the window again. Now Derrick was making the same expression, but he had put a finger up his nose, implying that not only was James an emotionless zombie, but a nose picker as well. Briefly, James wondered if whatever was changing Jenna was impacting Derrick as well. He quickly dismissed the idea, though. In fact, Derrick's behavior today was totally in keeping with his typical character.

James turned his attention back to the board. Mrs. Benson was explaining how cruel the Puritans could be and how readers were meant to sympathize with Hester, who was wrongfully judged and ostracized. And now Ella raised her hand to ask if the book had any truly likeable characters or if there were only a few sympathetic characters. James sympathized with Ella, who often faced ridicule for her work ethic. James's mother often told him that hard work always paid off, but that generalization had to be inaccurate.

James looked back at Derrick. Now he was making a different type of face. James couldn't be fully sure what it was, but he assumed that it was something obscene. James turned his eyes back towards the board. Mrs. Benson was talking to the class about the differences between laws and morals. James was looking forward, but he was focusing on the book on Derrick's desk. Derrick never took a notebook out, of course. Some of the football players made a genuine effort, but never Derrick. In fact, it seemed like Derrick made an effort to not display any effort. This meant that there was only the one small book to work with.

James focused on the book for a full minute before he allowed it to move. When it did, the book moved with a great deal of velocity. It hit corner-first into the ribs of one of the football players (James couldn't remember this one's name). The player brushed at his head and said, "What the hell, Derrick?"

This was the optimal result. James had been looking straight ahead, with Mrs. Benson looking directly at the class, confirming that he'd not performed any physical action. In addition, one of Derrick's teammates had cursed in class, and the apparent reason was that Derrick had hurled a book at him. Derrick's denials, though true, would only cast further suspicion upon him.

Sure enough, Mrs. Benson said, "Derrick, Andrew, what's going on?"

They were both quiet for a few seconds, but apparently Derrick figured out that someone had to be punished and decided that he would act first in order to protect himself. "Andrew cussed at me," he said.

Andrew opened and closed his mouth a few times before saying, "That's just because Derrick whipped his book at me for no reason."

"No, I didn't" Derrick yelled, but James could tell that he was looking at the book on the floor, wondering if he could grab it without getting caught. Sometimes, having a flat affect was a benefit. James could watch in amusement and anonymity.

"Well," Mrs. Benson said, "we'll have to figure out what the issue is after class. In the meantime, please do not disrupt my class again."

Mrs. Benson went back to talking about forgiveness and communities ganging up on people. The rest of the class snickered and whispered. James decided not to look in the window.

~ * ~

Harper had been listening to people's thoughts off and on the rest of the day. She hadn't done it very often since she'd first learned of her power. After most of a day, Harper had come to the conclusion that the other students were mostly creepy as hell. If they weren't obsessed with someone, then they wanted to hurt someone terribly, or they were planning on running away just so that they could become successful enough to come back and tell everyone to go to hell. High school was a very morbid place. Some of them, she could sympathize with. Boys would make roughly the same jokes about Alyssa as they would about her, just about giving her something more fun to ride than a wheelchair instead of making her walk straight. Others, like Brent, seemed angry with no real reason.

To make things even more frustrating, she hadn't found anyone whose thoughts sounded anything like Jenna's. In a way, that was good, because it meant that maybe things could be contained if it was just Jenna. Of course, Harper didn't know what "it" was well enough to know exactly how containing it would work. She supposed that she, James, and Krista should have expected that an abled student (a cruel one like Jenna in particular) might have had powers, but, up to this point, they'd really only kept an eye out for students with disabilities. Harper would put her radar up if she suspected anything.

Harper didn't want to admit it, but she was afraid to go into Jenna's head again. The hugeness and strangeness of it made it seem impossible to break through, like trying to learn a foreign language while being held underwater. But she knew that, eventually, she'd have to try again. If they were going to fight Jenna, they needed to know what she was and how she thought.

Harper got to her locker and set her bag down. She took the key on her necklace and opened the lock, then held the lock in her right hand, opening it with her left. When the door was open, she switched the lock back to her left hand and slid it into the latch on the locker. She started transferring the books she wouldn't need for home from her backpack to the locker. It would be a relatively light day in terms of actual homework, but between her history project and Jenna, it would be a long night full of worry.

Harper was just about to close up her locker when she heard someone thinking, "Help me." At first, Harper thought that somebody had actually said it out loud. It was so clear and so urgent that she could have sworn somebody said it while walking by, but when she turned away from her locker, nobody was looking around or panicking. Usually, to hear someone's thoughts, Harper had to will herself to look into their minds. This was a literal cry for help that someone had sent. But then why weren't they showing themselves? Was it a trick?

Harper looked more carefully up and down the hallway, but she still saw no sign of who it could be. Maybe whoever it was didn't even know that Harper could hear them. Maybe it was just a desperate call out to the universe. Maybe it was a few people thinking the same basic thing, overlapping.

Whatever it was, it had Harper rattled. She could feel herself shaking a little as she closed up her locker and zipped up her backpack. She made her way down the hall, trying to keep some kind of barrier of safety around her and, as always, failing. Today, though, she didn't notice the little bumps and stumbles like she usually did. Today, she just felt lost.

~ * ~

Today for lunch, Krista was having a bologna sandwich. She thought they were pretty gross, but it was the only lunch meat in the fridge, and they were out of peanut butter. "Maybe Jenna's tricking you," she told Harper.

Harper thought about it, then she shook her head. "I thought about that, but it felt too real."

Harper and Krista both looked at James, who had just taken a bite of his apple. He chewed before speaking. "Be careful not to link truly separate events."

"What does that mean?" Krista asked.

"What evidence do you have for your theory that Jenna is involved?"

"Um, Jenna's a demon?" Krista bit her sandwich. She tried to chew as little as possible before swallowing the lump down.

James shook his head. "You're thinking like a bad gambler."

Now Harper asked, "What does that mean?"

"Someone playing roulette might see two reds come up in a row and decide to bet on a black. This is wrong because each spin is its own unique event. The previous two don't affect the current one. Casinos rely on people not having sufficient understanding of probability to consistently take their money."

Krista took the bologna out of her sandwich, put it back in the baggie and ate what was now just a mustard sandwich. "I guess I'll never be rich."

"Of course," James said, "that doesn't prove that it was *not* Jenna. That's still very possible. It only means that we don't have sufficient evidence to decide yet."

"Great," Harper said. "Another thing to have to find out."

James took another bite of his apple. The three of them ate quietly for a bit. "And you haven't found anyone else in school whose mind sounds like Jenna's?" Krista asked.

"Not even close," Harper said. "I've listened to teachers, students, even that one weird hall monitor. I haven't picked up anything like her thoughts."

"Have you gone back in?" James asked.

Harper didn't answer at first, which was kind of an answer itself. When she did, it was after a long sigh. "Not yet. It's too much."

"We have to see what's going on," Krista said. "We have to stop Jenna."

"There is one thing," James said.

"Here we go," Krista said.

"No, really. We don't have any actual evidence that Jenna's mindset has made her evil. As far as we know, she hasn't *done* anything as of yet."

"She made me dizzy," Krista said. After puzzled looks from James and Harper, Krista explained what had happened in the locker room, then they were silent again for a bit.

Eventually, James said, "I know what to test. She saw Krista even when Krista was invisible. She seems to be resistant to Harper's listening. If she's resistant to me as well, then she's some kind of mirror image of us all. If I can exert power over her, then we know how to deal with her."

Harper nodded and Krista gave James a thumbs up. James looked over to Jenna's table. Today, she was chatting happily with the others there, acting like she was her usual self. James looked back down at the table. He decided to focus on the ends of her hair. James generally didn't move people's bodies, but he thought that hair would be light enough to manipulate.

James tried focusing on the end of her hair, but nothing seemed to happen. He closed his eyes and focused harder, just picturing a small patch of the end of her hairs by her left cheek. James started to hum quietly, but, still, nothing happened. James opened his eyes. "Well, we have a real problem."

Harper and Krista both looked over at Jenna quickly, but she

16

seemed to still not notice. Harper turned to James. "You sure?"

James sighed. He closed his eyes again and focused as hard as he could on the end of a single strand of hair. He simply pictured it for a few seconds before even trying to move it. When he felt that he had full hold of it, he pictured it rising. He saw the movement in his mind's eye, but he wasn't fully sure if it had moved or if it was a trick. Could Jenna be manipulating his mind? James opened his eyes quickly and looked at her. He wasn't fully sure what it was that he was seeing. "Krista, Harper," he said, "what does that expression mean?"

They were both quiet for a moment before speaking. Jenna's mouth had become a flat, thin line. "That expression," Krista said, "means that she's pissed."

~ * ~

After the locker-room incident, Krista had been cautious about turning invisible. Now, in the safety of her own room, she decided to try it again. She laid on her bed and looked at the ceiling. She let herself become invisible, then she got up and stood in front of the mirror. It always was a little disorienting at first, but once she pushed past that, Krista felt a kind of peace that she only felt while she was invisible. She felt fully herself when no one else was watching.

Krista put her hands to her face, feeling what she couldn't see. Next she lowered her hands a bit and touched her elbows, crossing her arms over her belly. She knew that her belly was a little too puffy, but there was comfort in feeling that it was hers.

Krista's thoughts were interrupted when her mother came into her room. Krista froze for a second, then slid into the corner near her closet. Her mother said, "Krista?" She looked around the room, shook her head, and mumbled a little. "Krista," she said, louder this time.

After not getting a reply, Krista's mother came into the room. She looked around a little. She looked under the bed. She went to Krista's dresser and opened the drawers, looking quickly in each one. Krista felt her heart beat faster. She knew there wasn't anything to hide, but she was surprised that her mom had enough interest to root through her things. After closing the top drawer, Krista's mom looked towards the closet. Krista did a quick look around her, making sure there was nothing in her way. Seeing that it was clear, Krista slid a couple of feet away, still staying close to the wall.

Sure enough, Krista's mom went to the closet. She opened the door and looked inside. Krista tried not to breathe too hard, tried not to fidget or do something else that her mother would catch but that she wouldn't be able to hear herself. Her mom leaned in a little, moved a few clothes around, and then said, "Ah, the hell with it." She closed the closet door and then sat on Krista's bed.

Krista was starting to get a Charley horse. She pumped her legs slowly and as softly as she possibly could. Her mom looked around the room, Krista wished that she had Harper there with her, but, of course, if Harper had been there, then she wouldn't be invisible. She thought that it was too bad that they couldn't find a way to share powers. As soon as the thought formed fully in her head, Krista gave a little gasp. Krista's mom looked in Krista's direction. She wasn't looking right in Krista's eyes, but definitely near her.

Krista tried to barely even breathe. She watched as her mother stood up, stretched, then left the room. She slid down to the ground, just staring forward. In front of her was nothing to see; it might as well have been herself.

~ * ~

Harper was doing her exercises and thinking. She tried to keep the fingers on her right hand straight as she pinched the small glob of Theraputty. There was always that bend in her fingers, no matter how hard she tried. But she was able to isolate relatively small clumps, bringing up smaller mounds in her Theraputty. She was getting a little better.

Unfortunately, Jenna was still an issue. If James could have some limited control over Jenna's body, then maybe there was some hope. Or maybe James had just caught her off guard, though even that would have given them some kind of idea of how to take her on. If they could get her off balance somehow, get her distracted, then they could have a real shot at her.

Harper realized that she had gotten distracted herself. The little mounds on her Theraputty had started to get larger and less regular. Harper used her left hand to flatten the Theraputty back out, and then she did five more good squeezes with her right hand. The problem with Jenna, Harper decided, was that nobody really knew what she wanted. She'd done a little intimidation and ridicule, but it wasn't that different from most of the popular kids in school. Just a little scarier, because it came in a new form.

Harper used her right hand to squeeze the Theraputty into a rough ball. She then switched over, putting her right hand flat and rolling it into a more perfect sphere. After it was spherical, she used her hand to flatten it. She tried to keep her fingers as straight as possible. She slid the flattened Theraputty back to the left and scrunched it back into a ball. Maybe part of the problem with Jenna was that they were viewing her as just pure evil instead of having some kind of specific goal. What if it was just that somebody at school liked Krista and Jenna was pissed off about it?

Harper thought about the boys in school. Up to this point, no boys had asked her to dance. Dylan had kind of flirted with her a couple of years ago, but it was hard to know if that was because he really liked her or if he was just after the notes that the teachers gave her in sixth grade so that she didn't have to type them up during class. But Harper had never given Dylan notes, and he was kind of a dick anyway, looking back.

Harper looked down at the Theraputty. She'd been using the green for almost two months. Her mom would never say anything, but Harper knew that she paid attention to those kinds of things. When she'd managed to switch from the bigger AFOs to the ankle-height braces, they'd had a "special dinner" to celebrate. Harper felt conflicted at best about that.

Harper wondered if she could peek into Jenna's mind for just long enough to get a feel for what she wanted. Like if you listened to a song in a foreign language, but you could still tell whether or not the singer was angry, sad, or happy. Harper picked up the Theraputty with both hands and twisted.

"Looking good, sweetie." It was Harper's dad.

"Thanks," she said. After she finished twisting, she set the Theraputty on her desk and rolled it into a smooth strand, making sure to incorporate her right hand.

"Getting hungry?" he asked. He had his hands together in front of him. Like a secret service agent.

"Getting there," she said. She'd always hated having her parents watching her do her therapy. They both would make suggestions, and the most frustrating part was that they both really believed that they were being helpful. She kept rolling the Theraputty instead of picking it up.

After a few quiet seconds, her father said, "Okay, then. Won't be long."

Harper waited for her father's footsteps to get quieter, then she picked up the Theraputty and twisted it slowly and carefully. She'd have to talk to Krista and James tomorrow.

~ * ~

Krista wasn't invisible, but she might as well have been. Standing behind two football players, a dance team member, and two other kids, Krista could hang back and just observe. She was waiting and watching for Jenna, for the moment when she would come in so that she could tell if Jenna was looking for her. With the other kids turned away from her, with no ability to read their lips, Krista got a vague sense of what they were saying and a few chunks of specifics. They were definitely making fun of Mrs. Benson, but for what, it was hard to say. Maybe it was her weight (she wasn't that fat, but weight was the usual angle for people to make fun of female teachers and students) or maybe it was just that she was boring (that one might have been a fairer point than the weight thing).

One of the football players turned around. His eyes went to Krista for just a second, then the football player looked further down the hall. Krista moved a bit to the left and slouched down a little. She decided not to look back at what the football player was looking at. Instead, she looked around, trying to find Jenna. She wasn't entirely sure if Jenna usually got to school early (to gossip with "friends" and belittle the less popular kids) or late (to show that she was too cool to be seen by the unwashed masses). And she was even less sure of whether the new Jenna would hold to whatever the original's pattern was.

Krista tried to keep looking around, hoping to catch Jenna without making it obvious that she was looking for someone. It wasn't unusual for her to scan the halls. She never trusted the hallway monitor to watch out for her. One of the few good lessons that her mother had taught her was to always be at least a little suspicious. Krista was just thinking about her mother going through her things when she saw Jenna.

Jenna was on her phone, seemingly oblivious to the world. Krista didn't really believe that, even if it wasn't evil that was driving the bus. Jenna was still able to walk through the stream of people in the hallway, though maybe that was just from years of practice. Krista pressed against the wall of lockers. She watched Jenna go by. She went slowly but steadily, never looking up or even to the side. When she was directly in front of the lockers that Krista was against, Jenna tilted her head up just slightly, then kept walking.

Over the years, Krista had learned to watch people's posture and movement. When you couldn't catch all of the words someone said, you had to watch their body language to get their general attitude. So Krista knew exactly what she had seen. It wasn't a random movement by Jenna. It wasn't even an attempt to sneak something past Krista. The signal had been absolutely clear. "I see you."

Krista nodded to herself. She felt like she was getting another piece of the puzzle. She knew now that Jenna had her monitor pretty much constantly up, but why was Krista being targeted? She would have to talk to Harper and James about the idea of combining powers somehow. She was worried that the other two might think that it was a dumb idea, but maybe James would be able to figure something out, and they had to stick together. It was always hard to be different, to not have a person to compare yourself to, but it was especially hard when you and your friends were trying to battle a possibly demonic glamor girl.

Krista made her way to her locker. There was no sense in getting flustered now. That was another nugget of wisdom from her mother. Her no good, snooping mother had taught her to barely care about most things.

When Krista got to her locker, she looked around again. It was hard not to get annoyed with the abled kids some days. Watching them take for granted their hearing, their legs, their neurotypical minds. There went some girls with high-heeled shoes, never thinking about Harper's problems. There went some of the stoners, burning away brain cells that others would love to have. She shook her head. It didn't do her any good to worry about it. It was just another of the many things in the category of "that's not fair." That seemed to be most of life.

~ * ~

James enjoyed watching the football players interact with each other today. After the fallout of the flying book in class, the two football players had been separated. The two had then actually stopped ridiculing James. They had both blamed the other for getting in trouble. Now, in the hall, the two of them called each other "retard" and "fag."

James thought carefully about what they were saying to each other. Obviously "retard" was a highly problematic term. Its imprecision was a major issue. While some might argue that the imprecision was simply a holdover from an earlier era and therefore not problematic, James could not agree. The problem with that view was that it failed to consider the fact that the imprecision of the term was part of the appeal to anyone using it. If the insulter really understood the struggle of who he was insulting, then it would make giving the insult harder. It would create too much empathy for insults to roll off the tongue.

This was just the first insult. The second insult, "fag," was also a problem, though a different one from James's perspective. James felt bad for the out kids in school. All day, they would hear "that's gay" or "fag" as insults, and they would have to ignore it, though a few of them would stand up to their antagonists now and then. James himself was genuinely conflicted. His father had frequently indicated that it was important to stand up for others when they were targeted. If a person was being isolated and ridiculed, then you had to help them. James's mother took the opposite position. She constantly told James that he should just not get involved one way or the other. His job was to stay safe.

James took what might be considered a middle view. One of the issues with defending people who would be categorized as "fags" was whether James's defense of them could actually be helpful. Given how much persecution James himself faced, he wasn't entirely sure that his defense of someone else would be an actual benefit to them instead of just a further reason for ridicule. Would James be more of a help or a problem?

James watched the football players punch each other in the arm. He supposed that it made a degree of sense. If affection was expressed through harshness and physical violence, then it made sense that they would antagonize everyone to whatever degree they could. In addition, if anyone objected, they could be ostracized, keeping the aggressors in a position of power. It was a logical but terrible way to make sure that they were always the model for popularity.

Now, the football players were pushing each other into lockers and laughing like utter imbeciles. As he watched them, James considered exerting his power. He could have easily increased the harshness of one of the pushes. When one of the football players crashed into a locker harder than he expected, he would almost certainly push his teammate as hard as he could. Things would start to escalate until a genuine fight broke out, and James would be able to feign total innocence. In fact, he likely would not have to feign anything. Nobody would think to make the accusation in the first place.

Of course, James did not follow through on this idea. Although there would be some pleasure in watching the two of them fight each other, this was different from the incident in class with the book. In that case, both of them were clearly antagonizing him. Here, while they were behaving badly, James could make no legitimate argument that their actions had an impact upon him one way or the other.

As James considered this, he wondered about how Jenna's mind worked. At this point in his life, James was fully aware of the fact that he did not think in neurotypical ways. Up to the current turn of events, James had every reason to assume that Jenna's mind was as "normal" as the majority of students in the school. But he realized now that might no longer be a safe assumption, if it ever had been. James began to wonder if she would register observations and process data in the same way that she had before. Perhaps not.

James was interrupted when somebody said, "What are you, a fag?"

James turned to see who it was. It was a short but solid boy. His name might have been Tony, though James could not remember for sure.

"That why you're staring?" the boy asked James. "Because you're a fag?"

"There's nothing wrong with gay people," James said. "But, no, that's not why I was staring."

The boy looked at James in an odd way. James wasn't sure if he was preparing for a physical assault or looking for a trait to ridicule. Without looking, James started to focus on the boy's right ankle, in case he needed to trip the boy.

But before anything else happened, the boy said, "Weirdo," and walked off. James watched the boy walk for a bit, making sure that he didn't turn around. When James was confident that the matter was ended, he headed off towards his own locker. He thought of his explanation of the casino to Krista and Harper. Were these related events, caused by Jenna? Events caused by whatever was impacting Jenna? Or was this a development that had been building for years, with every bit of ridicule and bullying for years? The possible depth of what they were facing made him feel slightly ill, and he knew that this was just the beginning. James knew that there would be much more to come.

~ * ~

The three of them were back at the lunch table. Today was hot dog day, which they all found disgusting. Krista still had to eat it sometime s, but today she had a bagel with some lunch meat. They were all comparing notes on aggression and anger in the school. After James told the girls about the fighting, Harper started telling them about changes in the feelings she had been picking up on. "I've tried to pinpoint where it's coming from," she said. "I expected it to be roving, following Jenna around the school, but it wasn't like that at all."

James nodded. "Up to this point, we have operated under the assumption that Jenna is the primary source of the disruptions, but that might not be the case."

"Did you find the spot where it's coming from?" Krista asked.

Harper sighed and held her water bottle with her right hand, trying not to squeeze it too much while she unscrewed it with her left. "Not really, or not in one specific place."

Krista peeled a little meat that was hanging off the side of her bagel. "I was thinking. She can always catch us coming individually. But maybe if we had James use his telepathy through Harper, or, if we could find a way to harness what I do along with Harper's power."

"I don't know if that's how things work," Harper said.

"We're also overlooking a practical issue," James said.

Krista ate the meat she peeled off. "And that is?"

"Even if we were able to subdue Jenna, what would we do with her?"

Harper said, "There has to be some place that we can hold her?"

"I don't have a mini prison at my house," Krista said.

James said, "Perhaps we should think of it less as a prison and more as a mobile hospital."

Harper took two carrot sticks out of a baggie. "Mobile hospital?"

"Something where we treat her even while she's on the move."

Two boys in the lunch line started yelling at each other. The three of them watched as one of the lunchroom monitors went over to break things up. Krista said, "What do you mean, 'treat'?"

The monitor made it over to the two boys. The boys listened for a minute, but as soon as the monitor walked away, they started pushing each other. James touched his ears, thinking. "If we could isolate the cause, maybe I could use telekinesis to trap it, to stop it?"

The boys had begun to grapple. The monitor turned back around to break it up again, but the "fight" chants had already started. Krista looked over towards Jenna. All smiling. Krista nudged James and Harper. They also looked over. "She's controlling them," Harper said.

"Quick," Krista said, "Go into one of their minds, Harper."

Harper looked over at them. Her face went blank for a moment. The monitor was speaking into her little walkie talkie when one of the boys landed a punch in the other's face. One of the other kids in line pulled the puncher off. Krista quickly looked over at Jenna. She was smiling and eating a potato chip, seemingly oblivious to the fight.

Harper shivered, then looked back at Krista and James. "Definitely

Jenna's work."

"What were their minds like?" James asked.

Harper shook her head. "It's not like Jenna's, but it's not like normal, either."

A couple of teachers were starting to come in, and the fight fully died down. The boys involved looked more lost than angry. "Was the rhythm of their thoughts like Jenna's?" James asked.

Harper considered this. "It's hard to say," she said. "Jenna's was so overwhelming that it was hard to get any real sense of its substance. This I could at least kind of get. It was just a little more chaotic than most people's."

Krista said, "Why did they fight?"

Harper half closed her eyes and paused a moment before speaking. "It's almost like they weren't really seeing each other. More like they were watching TV, but like they were channel surfing and every channel was screaming at them."

"A sensory overload?" James asked.

Harper shook her head. "It wasn't that so much. It was more that the constant change kept them from realizing that they were watching a show."

"So more like getting sucked into a comments thread on Facebook?" Krista said.

Harper laughed. She looked away from James and Krista. "Sort of. They won't really remember why they fought, so they'll get in trouble."

They started eating, not making much eye contact and not looking at Jenna. The lunchroom had settled down and they all felt a little drained. Eventually, James said, "This was a test."

"What do you mean?" Krista asked.

"I get it," Harper said. "She's seeing what she can get away with now so that she knows what her next move will be."

"Yes," James said. "That's what I think."

They were quiet again until Krista said, "Crap."

"Okay," Harper said. "Let's say that we do try to combine powers. How do we test it out?"

Krista said, "Can you go into James's mind as he tries to move something?"

Harper and James looked at the table. While Harper had been the one to form the trio, having looked into their minds, she'd made it a point to respect their privacy after that. "James," she said, "is that something you'd be okay with?"

James tilted his head a little and unfolded an empty baggie. "Do you think that you'd be able to isolate those thoughts? Only see my focus on moving something?"

"I can try?" Harper said. "I can't promise."

"Like you say, James," Krista said, "for the greater good."

"The greater good." James said.

They were quiet for a while, them. They sat picking at their lunches until Harper sighed and said, "We can try tomorrow, but we'll need to find a place."

~ * ~

Krista was going through her drawers, trying to imagine what her mother's reaction was to things. When she saw that there were tank tops, would she think that Krista was too fat for that kind of thing? When she saw the couple of thongs that Krista had, would she remember that she'd bought them for her, or would she just think that Krista was turning into a slut who saved up what little money she could get for sexy underwear? Or would her mother look at all the knock-offs and hand-me-downs and actually feel bad? That was hardest to imagine.

Krista closed the drawer again. She knew that she shouldn't let it get to her, but with the stuff with Jenna at school, with her mom's nagging at home, and now with her mom going through her things, it really felt like she had no safe place to be. Everywhere had a bully or a sneak that was looking to mess up her life. And that wasn't even counting the jerks that thought it was funny to make fun of her for being poor or hard of hearing.

Krista went and sat on her bed. She took the Shakespeare book they'd been assigned and tried to read it. They'd been assigned *Othello*. And over the list of characters, whoever had had the book last had written "interracial is hot." Krista wondered if there was some magical school some place where the boys weren't all immature jerks. It didn't seem likely. Krista read the first couple of pages of the play. She knew that she was supposed to appreciate Shakespeare's "mastery of language," but to be honest, Krista wasn't really sure what that meant. She kind of wondered if the schools that trained teachers to focus on finding newer and better ways of telling kids they were stupid and shouldn't be bored in class. Maybe that's what prepared them for real life.

Krista kept reading. She thought that Iago was a piece of crap, but she also thought that he'd get along with a lot of the jerks at school. He was such a nasty and heartless little turd that he'd fit right in at the right lunch table. After a while, Krista's eyes started to get tired. She rubbed them, and, when she opened them back up, her mother was there.

Krista dropped her book and put a hand on her chest. "God, Mom."

Her mom frowned. "What? I can't come into your room?"

Krista picked her book back up, closed it, and set it on her lap. "No, you just startled me."

Her mom popped a couple of M&Ms into her mouth. She must've been in a decent mood. "Well relax, I'm not going to yell at you. Just seeing how your day was."

Krista shrugged. "Boring. Yours?"

Her mom gave a little bit of a smile. "Yeah, about the same for me." She put a couple more M&Ms in her mouth. "How's school going?"

Krista tried not to change her facial expression. There was no reason to think that Jenna could extend her control all the way to Krista's house, but usually her mom would ask a question, get a one-word answer, then stumble away. "Like an unsharpened pencil."

Her mom squinted and chewed. "What?"

"Long and pointless."

Her mom nodded once, then she gave a single laugh. "Oh, I get it."

Krista smiled and watched her mom carefully. She tossed the rest of the M&Ms in her mouth. "Well, I'll let you get back to homework. Dinner in half an hour."

"Okay." Krista watched her mom walk out the door and down the hall. She wondered why she worried in the first place. Why would Jenna try to control her mom? Her mom couldn't do much of anything. Still, it had felt creepy for a little while. Krista wondered if she could get away with locking her door at night.

When Krista tried getting back into the book, she couldn't do it. She decided to put it away and work on math for a little bit. She could easily get through her problem set before dinner and finish reading after. Krista wondered why Harper bothered doing homework. She should be able to just screw off then use her powers to copy off one of the smart kids during the test. It was one of the many ways that she and Harper were different. And James was his whole other category of going to school. Krista tried not to be jealous of either Harper or James. With the other kids in school, it wasn't a big deal. But with these two, it felt like betrayal.

Krista stared at the problems on the worksheet. The first couple came easily enough. They were really the same problems that she'd seen done in class, just with different numbers. When she got about halfway through, though, the problems got harder, more complicated. Instead of doing the same things, she had to do the problems from the worksheet and some problem from a couple weeks ago. The trick was putting the problems in the right order, knowing which problem to do first. For once, math seemed like actual life.

~ * ~

A few days later, the school had gone from a minor level of tension to a heavy sense of doom. Krista was surprised that people reacted as strongly as they did. Tommy Russell hadn't been all that popular, so it wasn't like everyone's best friend had been in a car accident. And they had no real idea of what it would be like for him when he came back to school. She hated that all of the students thought that him possibly not being able to walk would be the worst curse ever. Of course, most of the students would see disability as tragic, or see him as a hero if he just came back to school. Tommy had basically been turned into a mascot that everyone was crying for. Almost everyone, anyway.

In the hallway, Krista saw Jenna. While most of the other kids probably thought that she just seemed drained, Krista recognized what Jenna was really feeling. Jenna was the most relaxed that Krista had ever seen her. What did this mean? Had Tommy started to figure something out about Jenna, so now he was gone? Or was she trying to show Harper, James, and Krista that bad things could happen even outside of school? Or was it just that the universe sucked?

Even apart from those questions, Krista felt shaken when Jenna walked past her and didn't even see her. At first, Krista thought that it was some kind of trick, like the morning that she'd tried to hide from Jenna. But as she watched Jenna keep walking, not breaking stride or turning her head, Krista realized that Jenna just didn't care. She didn't even seem to notice that she was stuck in high school, like the rest of the poor hallway zombies.

James saw Jenna in the hall, too. To him, she seemed blank, totally devoid of emotion. Sometimes, James knew that he just wasn't picking up a signal from the other students. This was different. With Jenna today, it seemed like there wasn't any signal for him to miss or misunderstand. He'd have to talk to Harper about it to be sure, but it seemed like there was an emptiness to Jenna.

Harper didn't actually see Jenna that morning, but she could tell. Like when someone opens a door and the temperature changes for a second. Harper just stared ahead and tried to walk straight. She didn't bother trying to look into Jenna's mind. Not right then, anyway. But she did try to get a sense of what it meant. Did this show that Jenna was weak and they should move on her, or was she stronger than ever? She tried to get a sense of what was happening with Jenna, but she couldn't do it. She couldn't do that and keep moving.

By the time that the three of them had gathered for lunch, they we re all both ready to do something and terrified to talk directly about it. Krista was the first to say something. "James," she said, "don't try telling us that there's no proof of what caused it."

"I looked at her," James said. "After looking at her, I will freely admit that there is sufficient evidence to feel suspicion. The deeper implication is the only question."

Krista had been waiting for a fight. When it didn't come, she just stared at James. After a bit of awkward silence, James shrugged and said, "What?"

"I tried to interpret whatever she was giving off," Harper said, "but it just felt disorienting. I couldn't quite sort through it."

"That's assuming there's something to get," James said.

"What do you mean?" Harper asked.

Krista laughed. "No, I get it. After all the times that I've joked about Jenna's head being empty, it might actually have come true."

"Not literally empty," James said.

"Thanks, James," Krista said. "That was very helpful."

James ignored her. He turned to Harper. "Did you try to actually go into her mind? I know that it's been difficult, but today is different."

Harper looked down at the table. "I'm…honestly, I'm scared."

"Don't try to do it directly," Krista said. "We need to find a way to tag team her."

"Tag team?" James said.

Krista ate a chip and thought. She was looking at the homecoming posters. Someone had put an Avengers picture on one, the text said, "Assemble at homecoming!" It was kind of sad and generic. "Let's say," Krista said, "that James focuses on Jenna's brain, not to crush it or anything, but to feel it, and then Harper watches his brain."

"Listens," Harper said.

"Whatever," Krista said. "The point is that maybe Jenna will catch James's tracking but miss Harper listening in." After a bit of silence, Krista said, "it's worth a try."

Harper looked at James and then back at the table. "James?" she asked. "Would that be okay?"

"I don't usually try to go inside of people. I've made inanimate objects inside of things move before, but I'm not entirely sure if the same principles apply."

"That's not what I meant," Harper said.

James was quiet for a moment. "I understand what you're asking, Harper. As we said before, it's for the greater good." He looked over to Jenna. She was eating her food without talking to any of the other kids at her table. "Is today a good day to try?" He asked.

Harper turned towards James. "Want to try?"

James gave a small nod. He tried to visualize Jenna's brain. When he was younger, James's parents had taken him to a number of

31

appointments where they had the models of people's brains. The skull was half full and fully covered, half open so that the brain was fully visible. James was fully aware that this model was only that; a model. But it gave him a framework to start with as he visualized Jenna's brain.

When it started to click for him, he gave another small nod. Harper listened to James's thoughts. She passed by the temptation to find some of the corners of his mind. Keeping a sense of trust was important and getting into Jenna's mind was even more important, so Harper tried to track James's thoughts as he pictured Jenna's brain. It was like trying to Skype on a weak signal. The first bit of tracking got mostly just noise. It was madness, but not quite as chaotic as Harper's first try at listening to Jenna's mind. This was hard, but fairly steady. Harper took a deep breath then she tried to focus more closely. It took a minute before she could get anything that she could understand, but once she heard it, she absolutely got it. Jenna was thinking, "I'm drowning."

Harper leaned back. "Oh my god, I heard her."

James closed his eyes. "I couldn't do it. I tried, but I lost it."

"I got it," Harper said. "The shocker? She needs help."

~ * ~

As Harper rode home in her mom's car, she practiced catching little snatches of thoughts. The guy walking his dog was picturing his boss on his knees, begging for help. In the man's fantasy he drove off, laughing at his boss's suffering. The old man at the corner worried about his cat. The mother with three kids was worried about getting home with enough time to make dinner. Harper was pleased. If she could jump from mind to mind, then maybe she could actually access Jenna's mind. It would be a matter of staying mentally nimble, of being able to switch channels quickly.

Deep down, though, she knew that it wasn't really Jenna's mind now. That sense was that she wasn't really in control, that she felt the panic of not really being able to breathe, suggested that the way to get rid of the school's problem was to break through the surface of whatever was holding her down. If they could do that, then they would be fighting it from both inside and out. The question, of course, was how to toss her a life preserver.

"Penny for your thoughts," Harper's mom said.

"A penny was the rate in your day, Mom. Kids today charge a dollar."

"Very funny, smart girl."

Harper wondered what her mom would think of what she was actually thinking about. She guessed that, if she was keeping things from her parents, then at least she was a normal teenager in one way. "The whole school seemed bummed out today," Harper said.

"I'm sure that everyone's shaken up when they heard about the accident," Harper's mom said. Harper waited for her mom to tell her that she could always talk if she needed someone to listen, but she didn't.

"Are you worried about me?" Harper asked.

"I'm the mother of a teenage girl," her mom said. "I'm always worried." They drove on in silence for a bit. Harper watched a couple on the sidewalk. The man was thinking about his job and if he might get fired. The woman was thinking about ice cream. "Were people talking about it at school?" Harper's mom asked.

Harper looked down at her hands. "Sort of," she said. "We didn't really talk about it because none of us really knew him, but what we talked about was kind of it. I don't know."

"No," her mom said. "I understand. You do lots of that as you become an adult."

They were quiet again. They passed a group of three boys walking down the street. Harper decided not to listen to their thoughts. The quiet in the car felt heavy, but not necessarily bad. "Mom," Harper said, "did you hate high school?"

Her mom was quiet for a full block, but Harper could tell that she was thinking, not just ignoring her. "I don't know if I hated it," her mom said. "But I remember all of the feelings that were stressful. The anxiety and the frustration. I remember that."

Harper was quiet, then she said, "It's kind of awful, but I don't know what would be any better than what we're stuck with."

Harper's mom laughed. "Being a parent. Being a parent is better than being in high school."

Harper looked at her mom's eyes in the rearview mirror. Her mom was smiling and watching the road. "Really?" Harper asked. "It's really better?"

"Definitely," her mom said. "Honey, I'm excited for all of the opportunities that you'll have, but I wouldn't wish to be back in high school."

"That's good to hear," Harper said.

"There are still frustrations," her mom said, "but it's different. You're more relaxed about it. Or maybe you're just too tired to care so much."

Harper and her mom both laughed a little. "I see the other kids at school," Harper said. "So many of them seem so angry. Or so depressed."

"How are you feeling?"

Harper considered the question honestly. A lot of the time, she would either ignore her mom's questions or joke her way past them, but this felt different. "I mean," she said. "I guess I'm as good as anyone else in the school. I don't feel like being mean like so many of them do. But I feel a sadness in the school. It's like it's hanging in the air, and that's what really scares me, I guess."

"Sadness because of the accident?"

Harper worried, for a second, about how honest she should be, but it seemed like a rare moment with her mom. "No," she said. "It's been there for a while."

They were quiet again, then her mom said, "And you know that this sadness is in the school, it's not something that's inside of you?"

"Yes," Harper said. "I know what it's like to be sad, Mom. This is different."

She heard her mom give a little sigh, and then her mom said, "Harper, I just want you to know that, if you ever need to talk, I'm waiting to listen."

"Thanks, Mom."

"And if you ever feel like you need someone else, if you don't want to just talk to your dad or me, we can find someone for you."

"Thanks, Mom." Harper looked out the window, but she quickly listened to her mother's mind. Her mom was thinking about what else to ask or if she should ask anything else. Harper felt bad for her mother. She was right to worry. She just didn't know about what. And how could Harper explain it to her? How could she make her understand?

~ * ~

"How would we use your invisibility?" James asked Krista.

"I don't know," she said. "Maybe if I make myself invisible, but you move my body, then I could attack her without getting caught?"

"Maybe I could try listening to her thoughts," Harper said. "While that distracts her, you could do something to her."

Krista looked over at Jenna's table. Jenna had lost her low-key blankness from yesterday. "I don't think it's just about distraction," Krista said. "It's kind of about masking, maybe, but I think it's more about coming together, building on each other."

"That's pretty touchy feely for you, Krista," Harper said.

"That doesn't mean she's wrong," said James.

Krista mimed pointing and laughing at Harper. Harper threw a grape at her. The three of them stopped talking for a bit. They ate and looked at Jenna on and off and at Ella on and off. Ella was bringing a card for Tommy for everyone to sign. She hadn't made it to their table yet. Krista wondered if that was intentional. She hadn't reached Jenna, either. Jenna's eyes were a little red and puffy, like she had been crying. But she was also talking a lot, and she smiled regularly. "Which one do you think Jenna's faking?" James asked.

"Which what?" Said Harper.

"Emotion," James said. "Do you think she's crying and just pretending to laugh, or is she pretending to laugh after really having cried?"

"Dang, James," Krista said. "That's profound."

"And hard to answer," Harper said. "It was hard to know what Jenna's real emotions were when she was just regular Jenna."

"If regular Jenna had actual emotions," Krista said.

Before anyone could say anything else, there was some noise at the far end of the lunch hall. Two boys, yelling, just like how the fight in the line had started. Almost immediately, there was yelling at the other end of the hall. The three of them all looked at Jenna. She was the only one at her table who wasn't watching the yelling. Instead, her face was turned down a little, as if there was something on the table. Her eyes looked wet, but she had the start of a smile.

"We still can't know what she's feeling or thinking." James said.

"I know," said Krista. "She's laughing at us and sending us a message. She heard us today, and she's letting us know that she can do two things at once."

"Then why is she crying?"

Harper answered. "Jenna's crying. She's crying because she's drowning and we can't save her. The thing that's holding her under is the thing that's laughing."

Krista shook her head. "I'll fight against the thing, but I still don't think that I can bring myself to fight to save Jenna."

Harper laughed. James asked, "That was a joke?"

Krista said, "It was about 64% of a joke."

The lunchroom monitors were starting to break up the fight on the far end of the lunch hall. The one on the near end, though, was starting to pick up steam. There was some yelling and then a big burst of laughter. The three of them looked over in time to see something remarkable. Darren Hodges, sophomore dork, mouthing off to one of the football team's defensive linemen, Brian Warren. Brian leaned in and started to yell at Darren, and then Darren pulled a fist back and punched him. Brian's head snapped back, and then his knees bent. He crumpled hard to the floor. There was a full second of silence, then it was a mix of screaming, yelling and laughing. People rushing to get a better view of the fight knocked over poor Ella.

"Any chance to trample the weak," Krista said. The crowd near the fight started to move. Half piled on top of Brian, still kicking and punching him. The other half went for Darren. Darren had been king of the lunch hall for less than fifteen seconds, and now he was being shoved to the floor and beaten.

"Okay," Krista said. "It's bad." She looked at Harper, then at James, and then she slipped under the table, where she turned invisible. James immediately began to focus on the people who had piled on Darren. As best as he could, James tried to slow them down, either tripping them as they kicked or pushing them over as they went to punch him. He had managed to push down or knock over five of the attackers when Jenna yelled. It was loud, and everything else stopped. Harper quickly listened for Krista's thoughts. She chuckled, then turned to James. "Krista nailed Jenna in the back of the head with a water bottle."

James raised his eyebrows. "Brave, but dangerous."

They both looked at Jenna. Her face was red. Her eyes were almost fully closed. "Well," James said, "I guess I don't need telepathy to know what she's thinking,"

"No," Harper said. "I guess you don't."

Krista came back, looking as though she walked back in from the bathroom. She was grinning from ear to ear. She sat down at the table and said, "Crisis averted."

"You'll pay for it, though." Harper said.

"Worth it," Krista said. She looked over at Jenna, who had picked up the bottle. She cracked it open and drank. Krista started laughing. "That's her comeback?"

Harper touched Krista's arm. "Don't push it."

Krista shrugged. "Maybe pushing her will make her screw up."

"It might not be worth taking that chance," James said.

"Aw, James," Krista said, "You do care.

They were quiet for a bit, and then Harper thought that James might have started to blush. The lunch hall had mostly quieted down and everyone was getting back to ordering and eating mediocre food. When Krista looked back at Jenna, Jenna's face had returned to its normal color. She took the bottle and poured the remaining water on the floor.

"A little better," Krista said, "but still kind of pathetic."

Jenna got up and walked away from her table. Just a few seconds later, another student walked by and slipped, both falling and dropping a tray of food on himself.

"You were saying?" James asked.

"Oh shut up," Krista said.

James raised his eyebrows. "Nice comeback."

~ * ~

After folding her clothes, Krista was positive that one of her socks was missing, but it seemed like such a pointless thing for her mom to have taken. It had to have been her mom. After she saw the sock was missing (after sorting through the usual pile of clean clothes that Krista's mom had dumped on her bed), Krista had gone back to the washer, the dryer, and the laundry basket. She'd checked under her bed and back in her drawer, in case it was already clean. It wasn't there. She stopped short of checking the trash.

The reasonable part of Krista's brain told her to quit worrying. It told her that this was just one missing sock, she should get over it. That part of her brain pointed out that the sock could have had a hole in it, and her mom could have thrown it away. But another part of her brain pointed out that her mom always just dumped Krista's clean clothes on her bed, and so she wouldn't have seen any hole in any sock.

Then there was one other part of Krista's brain. That part told her that the warning that Harper had given her was coming true. Somehow, her home was being invaded. But why a sock? The different parts of her brain continued to fight. Maybe the paranoia was Jenna's revenge and not the missing sock. But that thought didn't help things.

Krista gave a quick look at her bedroom door. Her mother wasn't around. Krista turned herself invisible and left her room. She kept looking around, as always, making sure that there was nothing to bump into or trip over, nothing to make noise and expose herself. She made her way to her mother's room. She steadied her breath (heavy breathing that she didn't hear herself had almost given her away some times before), and she went in. Her mom was in bed, watching TV. There was a drink on the little table by her bed. Krista's mom was watching *Cops*, though it was hard to tell how much she was actually watching it. Mostly, it looked like she was staring. After a few seconds, her mom reached over and grabbed her drink. She took a long sip without looking away from the TV screen, then she set the drink back down. She sniffed a little, then burped quietly.

Krista usually didn't feel much sympathy for her mother. She saw her drinking, saw her not going out to do things, she saw their crappy little home, and she thought of it all as things that her mom chose. Today, though, her mom looked like an animatronic statue. Like those moving statues at Chuck E. Cheese. It was sad, and it was creepy, but Krista knew that she couldn't let herself get sucked in. She took another step in, and she watched her mother. She didn't move. Krista looked around the room. Her mom had the lights off, so it was hard to see small things, sock-sized things. The floor had its usual piles of dirty clothes, but that was it. Her mom's dresser had a few jars and tubes of makeup and her lone bottle of ancient perfume. No clean clothes, and even if her mom was just drinking and staring, Krista wouldn't be able to actually open the drawer and look inside.

Krista took one more step inside. If she couldn't see anything, then she'd go back to her own room. Maybe she'd come back at a different time and poke around. After watching her mom for a few seconds (her mom took another drink), Krista looked around. In the corner, by her mother's closet, there was something balled up. It was impossible to tell what it was, and there was every chance that it was a piece of her mother's clothing, but Krista's heartbeat still started to speed up. The logical part of Krista's brain immediately explained it. Her mom had gone through her clean clothes, found one of Krista's socks, and tossed it into the corner. That was obviously that. No reason to freak out. That was assuming that it was Krista's sock, and she wasn't even sure of that much. It could also easily have been one of her mother's unmatched socks.

Krista looked down at her mom. She was sitting there, staring. Her eyelids were starting to droop. Usually, that was a good sign to Krista. Her mom was about to fall asleep, pass out or something else. After this, Krista could have her run of the house. Grab extra snacks, watch whatever she felt like watching, dance, whatever. But tonight, seeing her mom drift off as usual made Krista sad. She didn't pretend that it was just that she loved her mother or something. She knew that part of it was that she felt like she was seeing her own future. Maybe not the booze, but Krista worried about the loneliness and the general stink of defeat. What if she never moved out?

Krista's mom started laughing, and Krista jumped a little. She wasn't sure what was funny on *Cops*. Or maybe her mom had lost track of *Cops* and was laughing at something in her own head. Krista decided that she had to get out. She could look in the corner tomorrow. For now, Krista moved quickly but carefully back to her room. When she got there, she laid down on her bed and turned herself visible again. She stared up at the ceiling. Krista tried to remember if it had ever actually looked white or if it had always seemed kind of yellow. Maybe it had been like that when her mom and dad had moved in and her mom had always thought that she'd paint it later. Who knows? Maybe if Krista's dad was still around, they would have. There was no point in guessing now.

Krista sat up on the bed. She closed her eyes and breathed, willing herself not to cry. When Krista opened her eyes, she half expected her mother to be there, staring at Krista in the same blank way that she stared at her TV screen. But she wasn't there. It was just Krista. She got up and went to the kitchen. Krista looked down the hall. She could see the flickering from her mother's room. It was impossible to tell if her mom had woken back up or if she was dozing off again.

Krista exhaled. She went to the cupboard, found the bag of Oreos, and went back to her room. She could hear her mom's words, telling her not to get fat. Krista turned off her hearing aids, she opened the bag of Oreos, and she started to eat.

~ * ~

People didn't call James out for staring as much now as they had in years passed. He was sure that they talked about it, but the novelty of belittling him in front of everyone seemed to have worn off, so he could watch without having to hide it, and people would mutter without confronting him directly, James was fine with that. And so he watched Brent carefully, hiding in plain sight. Brent had the same slouch as usual, though he might have walked slightly slower. He still tended to look at the girls in the hall more than where he was actually headed. His backpack seemed mostly empty, too.

The football crew in general and Brent in particular seemed walled off, never showing interest in or even awareness of what was going on around them. It was only when Brent pushed past James in the hallway that James recognized something. Although it would have been easy to miss, Brent's lips were moving. James moved to the right and sped up, keeping pace with Brent. James couldn't be sure, but he thought that Brent was repeating something over and over. Like the chorus to a song. Or maybe it was the same chant that the football team was supposed to do to psych themselves up. But that didn't seem like Brent.

James was watching Brent so intently that he didn't notice the two other football players that came up to him until it was too late. Brian was one of them. Brian had a black eye and a swollen nose. "What are you staring at, queer?"

James looked at the two football players, then at Brent, who had turned on him. James pointed at Brent. "He bumped into me," he said. "He should say he's sorry."

Brent laughed. "You see," he said. "You let one chess dork punch you out, and all the geeks and fags are going to come after you."

Brent had stopped muttering but his eyes seemed strange, like he wasn't really looking at anything. "Better beat up this one, then. To make an example."

James knew he was in trouble, but he still tried to watch the football players, to see if they were working with Brent or just looking for someone to beat up. When they both stepped forward, they did it in unison. James backed away. "Really sorry. Probably my fault."

The push of students behind him made it impossible to get away. Instead the two football players grabbed him and shoved him up against the lockers. Brent walked over with his usual slow, uncaring gait. James struggled, but he knew what would happen. Brent stared at him for a few seconds, then shrugged and walked away. Each of the football players punched him in the gut once. As James doubled over, Brent walked back and bent down. He whispered, "Don't tell anybody, loser."

Both football players shoved James to the ground. They laughed as they walked off. Brent turned around to look at James. His lips were moving.

~ * ~

"So," James said, "we both have clear and immediate threats on us."

"Well," Harper said, "do we know that the threat on Krista is immediate?"

Krista said, "I guess my mom might just be screwing up the laundry. Not that her housekeeping skills were ever stellar."

"I was thinking more of Jenna," James said.

Krista said, "Oh, that."

They were all quiet. James wanted to continue the conversation, but he also recognized that he should give his friends some padding. He took a bite of his sandwich and waited for someone else to speak.

Harper went first. "Maybe I should piss someone off so I can join the club?"

"It might not come as naturally to you as it does to me," Krista said.

James looked at Harper, then Krista. They both appeared at ease. "There are at least two ways that we could approach these threats," he said. "The first would be to treat them as full, legitimate threats, and we would back off, waiting to do anything else until we felt safe."

"If we'll ever feel safe again," Krista said. She looked around the lunch hall. All the homecoming signs struck her as sad. They were almost all plain construction paper with dumb phrases written in marker. One of them said, "Brutal on the field, Smooth at the dance." Krista looked around, then grabbed it and pulled it off the wall. As she crumpled it up, she said, "We can't really stay away from the school. We're stuck here with it."

James said, "Which brings us to a second possible approach. If we assume that these threats are coming not because this thing is a threat to us, but because we are a threat to it, then we push harder."

"I like the idea," Harper said, "but how do we push?"

James said, "I noticed that Brent was moving his lips without really speaking."

"Maybe he was trying to read," Krista said.

"I suspect that he was chanting something," James said.

"Like a spell or something?" Harper asked.

James scratched his chin. "Well... a 'spell' might be a bit of a stretch. I'm not sure that getting two other football players to toss me around would take magic. I was thinking more like self-hypnosis."

"Self-hypnosis?" Krista said. "I know my hearing's not the best, but did you say 'self-hypnosis'?"

"You have a more reasonable explanation?"

Krista raised her hands. "They're all demons?"

"I'm not going to respond to that," James said.

Harper spoke. "Maybe we need to figure out how this is happening."

"They're demons being demony." Krista said.

"No," Harper said. "I mean, is whatever is controlling Jenna spreading? Is it getting bigger or is there a second thing now, and that second thing is inside Brent? Or is it transitioning out of Jenna and into Brent?"

They were quiet for a bit, and they each took turns looking over at Jenna. She was taking little sips from her Red Bull and not eating much. She looked more like regular Jenna than she had in a while.

"Maybe it has left her to go into Brent," James said.

"If it used Jenna, then left her for someone else, then this thing really does belong at the popular table," Krista said. Harper smiled but didn't laugh.

"Maybe it's a parasite," James said. "If it feeds on stress or despair, it would use Jenna until she was no longer useful, then it would find a new host."

"Like I said," Krista said. "It knows what table it belongs at."

"If that really is what it feeds on," Harper said, "then it seems like I'd be the ideal host."

Krista and James both stared at her. "What?" she said. "I would have the most direct access to everyone's thoughts and emotions, so I'd be the one that would get the most food."

"So much for you not facing a threat," Krista said.

James cocked his head to one side, then he set it straight again. "Jenna did seem to understand the nature of your powers. Or the thing inside her did."

Krista smiled. "I'm sure Jenna's had many things inside her."

"Potentially true," James said, "but not particularly helpful."

"I thought it helped to lighten the mood," Krista said.

"Listen," Harper said. "If I am the next target, if Brent is just a pit stop between Jenna and me, then you both understand what that means, right?"

Krista looked down at the table, but she nodded.

James said "It means that we have to watch you. It means that we can't just trust you to be you."

"Shouldn't that be for all three of us, though?" Krista asked.

"I don't think so," James said. "We all noted that Harper is the only one of us that has not received some kind of direct threat or intimidation. In other words, she's the one being encouraged to let her guard down."

"Great," said Krista, "So all we need to do is watch Harper for possession, attack Brent, keep an eye on Jenna all while trying to keep the school from collapsing."

"I would say 'infection' rather than 'possession', but other than that, yes."

Krista sighed. "You need to work on your sarcasm recognition, James."

"Or you could just be sarcastic less often."

"That's the most ridiculous suggestion of all," Krista said.

"Listen," Harper said, "I think that the first thing we need to do is find out more about this chant. We need to understand what it is that we're up against."

"So we do what?" Krista asked, "go to the library and ask for the 'demonic chants' section?"

James pointed at Krista. "Sarcasm," he said.

Before Krista could reply, Harper said, "I could try listening to Brent's thoughts. Maybe his will be less chaotic and overwhelming than when I tried with Jenna." They began to look around the lunch hall. Since Brent was an upperclassman, he wouldn't be there until later. But they did notice something. The room was quieter than usual. There was still some noise from people moving around and grabbing trays. But there was very little talking going on.

"So we're confident that this is all a matter of some horrible possession?" Harper asked.

"There is another possibility," James said.

Krista smiled a genuine smile. "James," she said, "of course there is."

James ignored her. "If there is some kind of transition going on from Jenna to Brent, then there might be a brief moment where neither one is really in control of anyone. If that is the case, then it would be that everyone is just feeling lost or uncertain with nobody really running things."

"The whole school is filled with sheep," Krista said. "How totally unsurprising." She looked over at Alyssa, sitting in her wheelchair a few tables over. She wondered if they should have invited her to their table earlier. It had never been intentional, but anybody could say the same thing.

"So now is an even better time to press forward?" Harper asked.

"Unless this is part of the whole 'false sense of security' plan to trick Harper," Krista said.

James sipped his water and thought. "That's not outside the realm of possibility, though the likelihood seems small to me, because then it seems less likely that we would face intimidation if it's trying to lull us into a sense of security."

Krista stared at James for a few seconds before turning to Harper. "Fine, but be careful, okay?"

Harper nodded. She appreciated both James's logical, steady push and Krista's concern. She'd need both of them if this was going to work. At least that much she knew.

~ * ~

"Are you going with anyone special?" Harper's mom asked.

"What? No, of course not. I wouldn't let someone pass a football game off as a date."

"Okay," her mom said. "I just was curious about your sudden interest in football, that's all."

"Not really football, Mom. I just thought I'd do something other than regular school."

"Sure," her mom said. "I understand." Harper was a little annoyed that her mom immediately wanted to invent a romantic life for her, but she also appreciated the easy cover. So, she just looked back out the window and sighed. A quick glance in the rearview mirror showed Harper that her mom was smiling. Harper supposed that it wasn't the worst thing ever, either, if her mom got to think that her daughter was having fun at school and developing a social life.

"So you'll need a ride?" her mom asked.

"Yes, please," Harper said. She wasn't sure if the "please" was too much. Her mom did look back at her quickly in the mirror, but then it was back to eyes on the road.

"Shouldn't be a problem," her mom said. "Do you have much homework tonight?"

Harper was glad for the shift in topic. "About the usual. A little math. Some reading. Some history."

"Sounds like fun."

Harper shrugged. "Could be worse. I heard that one of the AP English classes have to translate Beowulf from the old English."

Harper's mom said, "Well, that could be...yeah, I got nothing."

Harper and her mother laughed together. Harper thought about how different their conversations were compared to the conversations of even a few years ago. She couldn't settle on whether it was her fault or her mother's. It was more like gravity or the tides or something. It was just how things worked. Even Harper's mother had given her speeches about how she was at a point in her life when she was carving out her own identity. That had led to a whole awkward talk about how Harper's mom would try hard to be understanding when there was tension between them. Harper had just stared at her mother, wondering how she could think the conversation would be helpful in any way. When Harper listened to her mother's thoughts in that moment, she was horrified to realize that her mother was feeling proud of herself.

"Who is the football team playing, anyway?" Harper's mom asked.

Harper was glad that she'd actually made it a point to find this out. "East."

"Ooh," Harper's mom said. "That sounds like a big game."

"Yeah," Harper said, "I guess it'll give us bragging rights, though I'm not sure who we brag to."

"Those boys brag to each other," her mom said. "Most of sports is one group of boys explaining to another group of boys why their team is better and the other team is stupid. When they become adults, then beer is added."

Harper laughed again. "Well, at least it keeps them busy and mostly out of trouble."

"If only they could also argue about the best way to do dishes or something."

"Dad must be awfully stupid if he doesn't watch enough sports to argue with Uncle Jack."

Harper's mother gave a single laugh. "Of the issues that I have with your father, his relative lack of enthusiasm for sports on the weekend is not one of them."

Harper was quiet then, as was her mother. Harper wondered if her mother felt like she'd said more than she meant to. But, like her mother had done earlier, Harper changed topics. "Maybe we could have a debate about which of our mascots is cooler, though I doubt if the Tigers would come out on top."

"Are you kidding?" her mom asked. "They're grrreat."

"Oh Mom," Harper said, "I'd honestly rather talk sports than hear that joke again."

"Fine," her mom said. "I'll just go back to being horribly underappreciated as a humorist."

"Can I appreciate you as a mother, and we'll call it even?"

Harper's mother smiled. "I suppose that will do." They both sat quietly, then. It was pleasant, not having to anticipate what question might come next or read between the lines, "Honestly," Harper's mother said. "The Tigers are a much better symbol than what we used to have."

Harper sat silently for a few seconds, not even fully sure what she'd heard. "What do you mean?"

Harper's mom looked at her quickly in the rearview mirror. "You've heard this before."

"A different mascot? I don't think so."

"Sure you have," her mom said. "You know we used to be the Red Savages."

Harper laughed. She wasn't sure if her mom was being serious or not. "We actually were the Savages?"

"Our mascot's name was Sonny the Savage. He would put on a fake mohawk and war paint."

"Nobody ever said, 'this is horribly offensive and needs to be changed'?"

Harper's mom sighed. "I guess most people at the time didn't think it was such a big deal. I know that sounds stupid. It sounds that way when I say it now, but when you're raised seeing it..."

"Okay," Harper said. "I get it." After a pause, she said, "Did you ever think it was at least weird?"

"A lot," her mom said. "I'd see the kids at our school screaming, wearing some of that crap. And then there were the kids from the other schools. I don't even want to say the slurs they'd yell at games."

"I can't believe I never knew this."

"Well," her mom said, "we don't exactly advertise it these days. Sometimes, I think of all the senseless anger and ignorance. But when we were talking the other day, I don't know. I feel like it all seeped into the school's walls."

Harper shivered. This whole time, they'd imagined whatever they were fighting was housed in Jenna or Brent. They'd never thought that it could somehow be the school itself. Harper's mom chuckled. "Listen to me. Don't let me freak you out or anything. It's probably just me not liking high school."

"Well, I can't really blame you," Harper said. "There's plenty to dislike."

Harper regretted saying it when her mom asked, "Anything you want to talk about?"

"It's not that specific," Harper said. "Like you said. It's like it's in the building."

"I hope that home can feel safe for you, then." It was one of those statements that must have come off of a motivational poster and creeped into her mom's ear.

"Yeah," Harper said. "Definitely." It seemed like she should say more, but it also felt like there might be something in what her mom said that would be important even if it sounded dumb on the surface. Because Harper was still thinking it through, all she said was, "Sure beats school."

Her mom just sighed and said, "Good talk."

~ * ~

James shook his head. "I don't understand how it could actually be in the walls."

Harper shrugged. "Maybe it's not so much literally in the walls as it is just part of the school. Like maybe it's just been part of the student body for so long that we don't even notice it's there."

James nodded, but Harper could tell that he wasn't convinced. She looked over at Krista. Krista rolled her eyes, but she did give it a try. "You know how when you first go into one of the bio classrooms, there's that nasty smell of chemicals and dead things floating in jars?"

James frowned. "Formaldehyde is necessary for the preservation of specimens."

"But you know the smell, right?"

"Yes," James said, "I do know the smell, though, in all fairness, you do get used to it."

"Exactly," Krista said. "The smell's still there, but, after a while, you don't notice it."

James stared blankly for a moment, then he began to nod. "I see your point."

Krista pretended to give a bow and Harper gave a golf clap. "So," James eventually said, "this should impact how we approach Brent and Jenna."

"With fire," Krista said. Harper shot her a glance and Krista rolled her eyes again. They were quiet for a bit. Harper watched Ella as she was going from table to table, asking for suggestions for homecoming decorations or events, no doubt. Harper felt sorry for her, though the few times that she'd listened in to Ella's thoughts, Ella had never seemed sad.

"If it's the school itself," James said, "then it might make sense to try observing them away from here, trying to see if they're able to have any kind of freedom or relief."

"No way," Krista said, "if Jenna feels like she is drowning, then why would she come back to school instead of staying home or making her parents let her switch school?"

"That assumes that she understood the nature of what was happening," James said. "We've been watching and evaluating them, and we are still just hypothesizing about what's happening."

"He's got you there," Harper said. She looked over at Jenna. Jenna was staring off into space. She didn't even seem to notice the other people at the table. Harper half listened to Krista and James discussing whether or not they really understood what was happening. But she also started listening in to very small and very separate thoughts. Bio test Friday. Hair is getting long. Small and pointless thoughts. But eventually Harper picked up on something else. Something quiet and steady going on beneath all that. At first, Harper thought that maybe she was picking up someone else's thoughts, or even a song that was going through someone's head. It was so soothing that Harper found herself lost, staring off into nothing.

Harper wasn't sure how long she'd been staring off for when Krista started snapping her fingers in front of Harper's face. "Hello!" Krista said. "Earth to captain Ding Dong."

"Huh?" Harper blinked several times. She looked back and forth from Krista to James a couple of times. Then she looked back at Jenna. Jenna was now staring at the ceiling. She was twirling her hair with one hand. At first, Harper thought Jenna's mouth was hanging open, but then she realized that wasn't it. Jenna was chanting.

"Oh no," Harper said, "oh my God."

"What?" James asked. "What is it?"

Harper put her left hand over her mouth. She shook her head and fought back tears. When Harper took her hand away from her mouth, she took a deep breath and said, "James, you said a chant?"

"What?"

"Chanting, you said that you thought Brent was chanting under his breath, right?"

James reached up and touched his ear. "Yes, that was my reading of it."

"That's what I heard," Harper said. "Right now when I was staring off, the chant was how it got into my mind."

Krista put a hand up on Harper's right hand, which was tightly balled into a fist. "What do you mean? How did she get into your mind?

Did she hear what was going on in your mind?"

Harper thought about it carefully before answering. "Honestly, I don't know."

The three of them were quiet for a few minutes. Eventually, Krista said, "Damn." The other two nodded.

~ * ~

At the end of the day, James was watching the other students make their ways through the halls, looking for patterns. It was incredibly chaotic, but maybe if he could just pull back far enough, get a big picture view of things, then maybe he could start to see the repetition and connections. Maybe what Harper had said about the evil being in the student body could be clearly proven or disproven. Maybe they could learn something crucial. As it stood, James heard loudness and saw randomness. He saw high schoolers being high schoolers, which could either confirm or undercut the group's most recent theory about what was happening.

James looked up and down the hallway, watching for gaps. When he found one, he slipped in and went with the traffic. He watched his various classmates for signs of chanting or other repetitive behaviors. There was a lot of bumping and staring at phones, but nothing to really set him off. Then he saw Brent.

James slowed down as much as he could without getting trampled. Brent was moving fairly slowly, but if Brent was like Jenna, then he would be able to detect James without being right next to him, and James didn't want to be the victim of any more aggression. At the moment, Brent seemed unconcerned. James didn't have a clear view of his face, but Brent was carrying his backpack by one strap and talking to the players at his side. Every now and then, they would all laugh. Brent pointed at a girl with Down's syndrome and they all laughed, very hard.

James could feel in his head the urge to shove Brent. If he wanted, he should be able to pull one of Brent's shoes back, leaving him on the floor. James realized that, if he went to the football game with Harper, he'd be able to interfere with Brent's playing. He could push the ball to the ground after Brent threw it, maybe make Brent fumble. It might be interesting to see if whatever was controlling Brent would be angry if Brent's life got harder.

But in the hallway, it was probably a bad idea for James to go after Brent and James hadn't yet officially decided if he was going to the game or not. His parents had seemed oddly skeptical about him actually going. It had annoyed James, but he imagined that it was part of their larger anxiety about the way James interacted with his peers. He was sure that his decision would be analyzed and discussed in the coming days.

Brent and his friends had almost made it to the school doors. The doors had signs advertising the homecoming theme, which James found odd. Why did they need to actively remind people that they had made superheroes the homecoming theme? James sped up a bit, feeling safe. Right as Brent reached the door, he looked back at James. James tried to look away at first, but then he looked back up. The hallway traffic kept pushing James along and he would look at Brent, then look away. Brent had stepped to the side, letting other people go through the door. He was watching James and smirking.

"You got a problem, freak?" Brent asked.

James moved to the other side of the hall, keeping the traffic between himself and Brent. "You shouldn't make fun of people with disabilities. Will you make fun of Tommy when he comes back to school?"

Brent nodded. "Right," he said. "I'm sure you tards have to stick together, right?"

"You're the one who should be embarrassed here," James said.

Brent looked back at the people walking down the hall. "Yeah," he said, "I'm sure that everyone in school thinks I'm the weirdo."

James said, "Just because most people cling to something, that doesn't make it right." Then he slipped back into the traffic and went out the door before Brent could respond. He tried to calm himself so that he could reflect effectively on what had just happened. It seemed like typical Brent, but the fact that Brent knew to look back at James made him suspect that it wasn't quite so simple. James felt that this thing was unsettling them more than they unsettled it.

~ * ~

Krista was the last one to make it to the game. The three of them met a little ways past the gate. "Sorry," Krista said. "I had to walk here."

"My mom would've given you a ride," Harper said.

Krista shook her head. "Don't worry. But maybe for the way home."

"Where should we sit?" James asked. They looked at the stands, which were moderately full. The top of the bleachers was mostly students, the lower section had mostly families.

"Not too close to the band," Krista said. "I won't be able to catch anything you say."

"We could always sit in the visitors' section," James said.

Krista laughed. "That would feel right. Probably better than in the home section."

"No," Harper said. "We can't risk drawing attention to ourselves."

They were quiet for a bit, scanning the stands. Then James said, "There," pointing to a mostly empty section.

"Won't that leave us kind of exposed?" Harper asked.

"Look closer," James said. "The two families on the left are both saving seats."

As Harper and Krista looked, they saw that he was right. There were a couple of jackets and seat cushions laid out. "If we sit near them," James said, "we'll blend in when their friends come, but we'll also be a bit isolated. We'll still be able to talk."

"Good eye, James," Krista said.

James gave a small smile. "Anyone want popcorn before we take our seats?"

"Popcorn?" Harper said. "James, I feel like throwing up."

"I'll take a soda," Krista said. After Harper glared at her, Krista said, "What? If we're going to die, we might as well enjoy our last moments, and I'd like a soda.

"One soda," James said. "I'll get that, and you can go get seats." James went towards the concession stand, and Krista shrugged and held her arm out to Harper. Harper smiled and put her arm under Krista's. "Maybe we can look out for cute boys," Krista said. "You know, in case we don't die."

Harper let herself laugh. She really did feel scared, but she didn't want to let herself shut down. Harper wasn't entirely sure about the mechanics of her power, but she knew that, when she was listening to someone else's thoughts, she felt somehow outside of herself. It was one of the things that she enjoyed most about her power. If she was too wrapped up in her own fear, then she might not be able to go into Brent's mind. "Do you think you could sense the invisible thing, the entity controlling all of us, if we were close to it?" Harper asked Krista. "Do you think you could pick up on it?"

Krista was quiet for a bit. At first, Harper thought maybe she hadn't heard her. She was about to ask again when Krista said, "Honestly, I don't really know what I'd be looking for."

They got to the steps for the bleachers, and Krista looked over at Harper. "Need help?"

"Sure," Harper said. Krista stood on Harper's right side, and they went up the left side of the stairs so that Harper could hold onto the rail with her dominant hand. They hadn't gotten more than a few steps up when the first set of students started coming down the bleachers on the same side Harper and Krista were going up. The students stopped and said, "Excuse you."

Krista stepped up, "Excuse you. We need to use this side, you don't."

The front student looked at her two friends and gave one laugh. "Why do you have to?"

Krista narrowed her eyes. "We're British and it's our culture. Why do you think, moron?"

All three girls laughed and pushed past Krista, bumping into her. After they went past, Krista turned to Harper. "They were just jackasses."

"Don't worry about them," Harper said. She started making her way up again. When they were almost all the way at the top of the stairs, they ran into an older couple. The husband said, "Oh, pardon me."

Harper and Krista laughed with each other. Krista moved to the side, and the couple squeezed between Harper and Krista. They moved forward and made their way towards the middle of the bleachers. They got to the seats James had pointed to and sat. One of the families was wearing Tigers gear. Krista looked at Harper, smiling, but Harper shook her head, and they just sat down.

"This is weird," said Krista. Harper nodded. On the field, the football players were doing some kind of drill that involved short bursts of running. "Looks like PE class," Krista said.

When Harper spoke, she did so quietly, but she enunciated carefully so that Krista could read her lips. "Gotta do what you're good at. That's why we do classes instead."

"You're good at classes," Krista said. "All I've got is sarcasm."

Harper rolled her eyes, but she realized that she didn't really know much about Krista's academic performance. They'd originally started talking because Harper had been searching through people's minds and she was happy to find someone else with a power. She'd gotten a little sense of what Krista's home life was like, and they'd talked about what teachers they liked or disliked, but there was a lot about Krista and James that she assumed without really knowing.

"There's James," Krista said. James had two sodas and a popcorn. He made his way to Krista and Harper. He nodded and sat down. "Anything exciting happen yet?" he asked.

"Not yet," Harper said, "but Brent is out on the field, and Jenna must be here somewhere."

James handed Krista one of the sodas. "Let's wait until the game starts to try anything."

"Agreed," Harper said. "Let's go big so that we can get a significant emotional reaction."

James sat down. "I was thinking I'd try to trip him on a pass play, something simple."

Krista leaned in. "I missed that."

Harper put her right hand as flat as she could, then she made her index and middle fingers of her left hand look like a pair of legs. She then had the legs crumple. Krista nodded.

"When should I go off to poke around?" she asked.

James said, "I would move in the second quarter. People will be paying attention to the game and there will be minimal traffic since people will decide to wait for half-time to get up."

Krista nodded. The three of them watched the teams finish their warm ups. They gave a small bit of applause during the player introductions. The Tigers were on defense first, so the three of them just watched. By the end of the first quarter, they were all getting antsy, and so was the crowd. The Tigers scored a touchdown, and then East got their second field goal of the game. James observed, not interfering. Since then, the Tigers had to punt, and East was driving. "When are we doing something?" Krista asked.

Harper looked over to James. James started to rub the back of his neck. "I can't do anything until they get the ball again. Ditto for Harper. If you want to try something, you can, but you need to be incredibly careful. Everyone here is on edge right now."

Krista nodded. She started to get up, and Harper touched her arm. Krista stopped and looked Harper directly in the eye. Harper said, "We mean it. You can't afford to not take this seriously."

Krista was quiet, then she said, "My family is poor. I can't really afford much of anything."

She got up and left before Harper could say anything else. After some silence, she moved closer to James. "She'll be okay," Harper asked, "right?"

"Honestly?"

Harper thought about it. "No," she said. "In this case, it would probably be best to just lie."

James stared at the field. An East player slipped and fell, missing a chance to make a first down. "She'll be fine," James said. "Everything will work out tonight."

Harper sighed. "Well, if the Tigers can stop them here, then we'll be up, too."

East broke out of their huddle and went up to the line. James and Harper were holding their breath watching, the same as everyone else, just for different reasons. East snapped the ball, and the quarterback dropped back. He looked down the field, paused, then threw. The ball went to one of the East players. It hit him almost perfectly in the hands, but he dropped it. The roar from the stands was huge. After it quieted down, Harper leaned over to James. "Was that you?"

James shook his head. "No, this time somebody just blew it on their own."

Harper nodded. East punted the ball, and the Tiger player who caught the ball was able to gain a few yards before being tackled. As the Tigers offense came on the field, Harper leaned in towards James again. "So the first pass play, you'll mess with Brent and I'll listen to his thoughts?"

James nodded and kept his face turned towards the field. The crowd was cheering loudly as the Tigers went up to the line. Harper realized that she was holding her breath and she forced herself to exhale. James looked like a statue, no real expression, just rocking slightly. The first play was a run, and it only got a couple yards. Part of the crowd clapped, a bigger part groaned, and most just stayed silent. The second play was another run. It also only got about two yards. "Oh come on," Harper said.

One of the people sitting near her looked over and smiled. "Don't worry, sweetie," she said. "The Tigers will pull it off, just you wait."

Harper laughed at herself. "You're right," she said, "I just got sucked into the game."

"That's why we're here, right?" the woman said.

Harper looked at James. He might have been smiling a little, but it was hard to tell. Harper wondered about the woman who had spoken to her. Had she gone to this school? Had she ever cheered for the Savages?

James leaned over and quietly said, "Here we go."

Sure enough, Brent dropped back. It was a pass play. James pictured the front tip of the ball, which was difficult, because it was in motion. Harper listened carefully to Brent's mind. Brent was watching the receivers and tracking where they'd be. There was no chanting or anything else. He was actually focused on the game, or he was trying to anyway. Every so often, something would kind of jam his thinking. James watched the ball, keeping his eye on the front end. When Brent pulled his arm back and started to throw, James pushed against it, lightly. It didn't stop the ball, but it did tip it, making the ball pitch down. Instead of making it to the receiver, the ball ended up hitting one of the lineman's helmets. It bounced off and fell to the ground. Brent stared at it.

There was silence for a moment, and then Harper heard a string of obscenities go through Brent's mind, though he couldn't follow all the way through on any sentence he started. Was that the thing in the school or just his nerves? She actually felt a little bad for Brent, which surprised Harper. But then she had a thought. She grabbed James's arm, "Help him," she said.

James leaned in. "I must've misheard you. What did you say?"

"Help Brent have the game of his life. The thing isn't controlling him right now. Not like usual, anyway. I want you to make sure that he has a good rest of the game."

James didn't answer. Instead, he turned back to the game. The Tigers punted. It was a medium kick, but the East returner dropped the ball. The ball bounced forward and one of the Tigers players was able to recover it. James said, "I hope you know what we're doing."

The Tigers made a slow but steady drive down the field and scored a touchdown after an East player stumbled without tackling the running back. All the while, Harper kept listening to Brent's thoughts. He was happy. The whole drive, he seemed excited, but also at peace. Harper decided to keep listening when he came off the field. After he was on the sidelines for a couple of minutes, Harper could hear it again. It was faint, but it was there. The chanting.

Harper quickly snapped out of Brent's mind and looked over at James. James looked pale.

"Are you okay?" she asked him, touching his shoulder.

James turned his head towards her very slowly. "It's a lot," he said. After Harper didn't react, he said, "I'm not used to doing this much all at once."

Harper gave his shoulder a squeeze. "Don't overdo it. Do only as much as you can." James shrugged off her hand and massaged his temples. Harper said, "Really, it's probably best if you don't do too much anyway. We don't want people to notice what's happening."

"Stimulation," James said. "There's so much noise here."

Harper realized how much of tonight she hadn't really thought through. She hoped that Krista was okay. "Just relax through half-time," she said. "I'm sure it will be okay."

Sure enough, East drove a little way but didn't get much past mid field before the end of the second quarter. James was definitely looking better, but he said, "I'm going to walk around."

Harper didn't try to stop him. She sat in the stands and thought about what Brent's clear mind might mean. It took her a minute to realize the woman in the stands was talking to her again.

"I said," the woman said, "are you and your friend going through some problems?"

Harper tried not to laugh. "No. Or, not romantic problems anyway."

The old woman nodded, but like she didn't believe Harper. "Well," the woman said. "I'm sure that the two of you'll be able to figure it out one way or the other."

"Thanks," Harper said. "I sure hope so." She actually felt grateful for being single, something she didn't feel very often. But right now, there was way too much to manage without a boyfriend. When James got back, Harper smiled at him. "Feeling better?"

James sat down without directly looking at Harper. "Much better than before, certainly."

Harper looked over at the old woman, who smiled and gave her a thumbs up. Harper leaned in towards James. "They should be in good shape, so only help if it looks like they're going to be in trouble."

James nodded. The second half started with the Tigers receiving. They had another slow but steady drive down the field, with a touchdown coming on a pass play. The ball wobbled a little after leaving Brent's hands, but it steadied itself and the receiver caught it. After the cheering had died down, Harper asked James if he was all right. James nodded. "Fine," he said. "I'm fine." Harper realized that she was acting like her mother, and she stopped talking to James.

East was a few plays into a drive when Krista came back. She was holding something in her right hand, but neither James nor Harper could see what it was. Harper asked Krista what she had, but Krista seemed to not hear. A couple of plays later, an East player was able to break away, and it looked like he might be headed for a touchdown, but he slipped and fell hard to the ground. Krista looked over at James. "What, are you working for the enemy, now?"

James pointed to Harper. "Boss's orders," he said. "And technically

East is the enemy."

"Not from where I'm sitting." Krista said.

"You're sitting in the home section."

Krista rolled her eyes. "Good God, James, let me have my complaints. They're all I have."

James shrugged. "Just trying to be correct."

Before Krista could respond, Harper asked her, "What did you find out?"

Krista leaned in. "Well, for starters, I can say that guys' locker rooms are disgusting."

James said, "My PE experiences allow me to confirm this."

Harper chuckled, "I'm glad that you two are back on the same page, but I was looking for something that might actually help us at some point."

"There's more," Krista said. "I was keeping an eye on Brent in the locker room. At first the coach was talking to him. Well, yelling, really. But after all that, the coach went to yell at some other players. The defense, I think. I kept watching Brent, and I noticed his lips moving."

"He was chanting." James said.

"That's what I figured at first too," Krista said. "So I tried reading his lips to see what he was saying. At first, I thought it was gibberish, but then I realized he was saying colors and numbers."

"A code?" James asked. "Maybe he's transmitting information to control other players?"

Krista shook her head. "I don't think he was hypnotizing anyone. It looked more like he was trying to make sure that he would remember something."

"That could still be a code," James said. They were interrupted by a larger roar from the crowd. The Tigers had just received a fumble. The three of them watched quietly as the team's players exited and entered the field. "Who would Brent be remembering code for?" James asked.

Harper watched the Tigers go from the huddle to the line. As Brent started yelling, Harper said, "I think he's remembering the code for the other football players."

James frowned. "Krista said he wasn't trying to control anyone."

"No," Harper said, "I think he was trying to remember the names for their plays."

~ * ~

After the game, Harper and Krista were standing by a tree at the edge of the parking lot, looking for Harper's mom's car. The Tigers had won 34 to 17 with minimal help from James in the second half. Maybe the confidence boost from his initial help was enough. "Thanks for asking for a ride for me," Krista said.

"No problem," Harper said. "My mom will be happy to have evidence that I actually do have friends."

Krista laughed. "Sorry it couldn't be someone from the cool kid's table."

"Nah," Harper said. "That would just make her suspicious." They were quiet for a bit, watching some of their classmates pass by, chanting, "Let's go Tigers." Krista rolled her eyes and Harper laughed. The next group to walk by was the old woman that had been sitting near the three of them. She seemed to notice Harper right away and she smiled. "See," she said, "I knew you guys would figure it out, and you did."

Harper raised her eyebrows. "Excuse me?"

The old woman kept smiling, but her eyes looked hard. "I know that you figured it out. That's all. And we might have figured something out, too."

Her friends had kept going and the old woman turned to catch up to them. "Dang," Krista said. "Creep much, old lady?" Harper didn't reply at first. She just stared after the old woman. By the time she and her friends got to their car the woman seemed to be laughing naturally, kindly. "It doesn't matter," Harper said. "Just another little weird something, but it'll pass."

Krista said, "What?"

Harper just shook her head. She spoke slowly and clearly. "Let's go find my mom." Krista nodded and they went off into the parking lot. Cars were moving slowly, with students driving in and out between them. It was a wonder that no one got hurt. "There," Harper said.

They went over to the car. Harper went to her mom's window. Her mom rolled the window down and said, "So, it looks like we won?"

Harper laughed. "Yeah, we beat those jerks. Can we give my friend a ride home?"

Harper's mom looked over Harper's shoulder at Krista. Krista waved shyly. Harper listened to her mom's thoughts for just a few seconds, to make sure everything was okay. It was. Like she'd thought, her mom was happy for her. "Sure," she said. "Get in."

Both girls got in. Krista said, "Hi, thanks for the ride."

Harper's mom said, "No problem," and they all settled in to an awkward silence. Harper realized that most of the talking that she and Krista did centered around whatever was running the school, whatever was controlling Jenna and Brent and, apparently, some old woman in the parking lot.

Harper's mom said, "So, was the game exciting?"

Harper answered, not sure how well Krista heard. "Yeah, it was a fun game to watch."

Harper looked over at Krista, she looked amused enough that Harper figured that she must have heard what Harper had said, even if she didn't catch the full question.

"Krista," Harper's mom said, "are you a football fan?"

After a "What?" from Krista and a louder repetition of the question from Harper's mom, Krista said, "Less of a football fan and more of a not-spending-Friday-night-at-home fan."

Harper's mom laughed. "I'm sure that's a very big fan club for your age."

Krista smiled. Harper thought about listening into her thoughts, but she decided against it. After a little pause, Krista said, "That might be about the only way I'm like the other kids at school."

"The more normal, the less special," Harper's mom said.

Krista looked over at Harper. Harper said, "That's what my mom and dad always say about me."

Krista nodded. "That's sweet." Harper couldn't tell if Krista was making fun of her family or not.

"Where do you live?" Harper's mom asked. Krista gave the directions, and Harper realized that, not only had she never been to Krista's house, she wasn't even totally sure of what part of town Krista lived in. She felt bad. "You should come over for dinner sometime," Harper said.

Krista looked at Harper. She looked stunned, but Harper's mom said, "Yeah, you're always welcome."

It was too dark to be sure, but Harper was almost positive that Krista was blushing. Harper might not have believed it if she hadn't mostly seen it. "Thanks," Krista said, "that's kind of you."

The rest of the ride home was fairly pleasant. They kept discussion going without really getting too personal. When they got to Krista's house, she thanked Harper's mom multiple times and got out quickly. She went to her door and waved goodbye. Harper's mom backed out of the driveway. She spoke without turning around. "She seemed nice."

"She is," Harper said. "She really is."

~ * ~

James had agreed to go with his family to the grocery store. Once at the store, James had agreed to pick out produce. His eye for detail helped him to pick out the best produce that was the right combination of ripe and able to last. He was sorting through the onions, checking for color and firmness, when he saw something that startled him. It was Brent.

"James," Brent said. He was looking in James's general direction without making direct eye contact. "I really hope that you enjoyed the game."

James pressed an onion to his chest and looked at the floor, "Game?" he asked.

Brent gave a single, quiet laugh. "Don't worry about it then, I guess."

James put his onion back on the pile. Brent looked around. "Look, I'm sorry about calling you a tard the other day." When James didn't reply, Brent finally looked directly at his face. "Okay," he said. "I just wanted to say that, like, I knew you three were at the game or whatever, and I don't know. I don't know why, but it's like I'm supposed to thank you or something."

After a pause, James said, "Yes, I think that I know what you're talking about."

Brent looked away again. "Yeah, right. Well, I don't know. Hey, don't tell anyone in school about this, okay?"

James gave a single quick nod. He thought about asking Brent about the entity. It seemed like he had some idea that something was going on, but not a deep understanding. Could Brent be pretending? Could it be a trap? James just picked up another onion, feeling its weight and squishiness between his fingers.

Brent said, "Well, I'll see you Monday, then. Back in school," and he walked away. James watched him turn down an aisle. The last statement felt particularly ominous. The clear implication was that, on Monday, Brent would be back under the thing's control. Perhaps he'd have no memory of James's help during the game or even of this conversation in the store. James finished with the onions and moved on to fruit.

James did consider the possibility that all of this was a ruse. Brent might not be acting as Brent after all, and this might be meant to make James paranoid, to distract him, or to otherwise confuse him. James looked down at the peaches. He hated them. Their fuzz was agitating. But, when given a disagreeable task, it was usually best to proceed immediately and efficiently. Perhaps that was the way to deal with Brent: quickly but carefully. James tried to look over the peaches, judging them shrewdly on color so he wouldn't have to feel them too much. He reached down to grab a particularly red peach, but he withdrew his hand immediately. It was both fuzzy and overly firm. James was not one to trust omens, but this didn't give him confidence.

James looked around the produce section. He wished that Harper was with him. She would be able to track Brent, to see what he was really thinking. James could only move things. He supposed that Harper, with her physical issues, might envy him. James wondered then if he should feel bad for thinking such a thing. Harper would definitely tell him not to feel bad, that he was being logical (which, in all fairness, he was), but Krista would certainly tell him that he was a jerk. Or worse. Though it was hard to say if she would have believed it or if she would have just been having fun. Besides, this was all purely hypothetical anyway.

James looked down at a peach. He focused on the pit inside instead of the skin or the flesh. He put a plastic bag in the bin with the peaches, and he watched this peach roll into the bag. Once it was inside the bag, he felt it, lightly. It was indeed, soft enough. James looked around the produce section again. No one was watching him. James used his power to bring in two more peaches. He felt calm. More calm and content than he'd felt in quite some time.

~ * ~

James had finished telling Krista and Harper about seeing Brent in the store. Krista looked over at Jenna. She was crying, and half of her table seemed to be comforting her and half seemed to be gossiping about her.

James asked Harper, "Do you think you could listen to Brent's mind from here?"

Harper shook her head. "I don't know where he is, so I don't think I'd be able to figure out who I was actually listening to. I mean, maybe I'd recognize the thing, but I can't be sure. I might end up accidentally listening to someone else's thoughts or even getting sucked into another possessed person's thoughts."

Jenna had a hand over her eyes, and she was talking. Her head was tilted down, so Krista couldn't read her lips. But the two groups of friends, the gossipers and the listeners, were starting to talk to each other. Krista could almost see Jenna's control over everyone slipping away. As much as she enjoyed thinking about Jenna getting dumped by the evil spirit and her friends all at once, she did feel a little bad. How much control did Jenna have?

"Maybe after school?" James asked. "He's always taking his time down the hallway."

"Maybe," Harper said. "But someone should stick close. Keep an eye on me so I don't get sucked in."

"What about Jenna?" Krista asked. "What's up with her today?"

Harper and James looked at Jenna. Some of the side gossipers were starting to laugh with each other. It didn't seem like Jenna noticed. "This is definitely unusual behavior," James said.

"Do you think that I should try listening to her thoughts?" Harper asked.

They were quiet for a moment. It was so hard to determine what was important and what was just game playing. Nobody seemed to want to talk first, so Krista said, "Do it. Let's see what's going on."

Harper looked to James. He gave a shrug, then a nod. Harper looked over at Jenna. Krista and James watched Harper's face while she listened. At first, it went blank, with Harper staring off. Then, the corners of her mouth turned down, and her eyes started to squint shut. Krista grabbed Harper's left arm and shook it. Harper jumped a little.

"Holy crap," Krista said. "What was that all about?"

Harper looked from Krista to James. She started blushing and sweat beads formed on her forehead. "What?"

"You looked very upset," James said. "Maybe even more than Jenna does."

"I don't really," Harper stopped and frowned. "I know that I was in there. I know she felt sad."

"We kind of gathered that from the sobbing and stuff," Krista said.

"That sarcasm was a bit harsh," James said, "but it does accurately portray my lack of surprise."

"It was also hilarious," Krista said. When the other two looked at her, she said, "Comic relief is helpful."

"Does this mean that she's still most likely drowning?" James asked.

Harper closed her eyes. "Not like she had been," she said. "It could be that she's being shielded somehow. That whatever was in control of her before is acting as a barrier to me now. Or it could be that the only thing that's left is emptiness."

"Or it could be a trap," James said. "Presenting as being harmless or vulnerable is a good way to draw someone in."

"That makes sense," Harper said. "It's already tried to pull me in once."

"She doesn't seem to have noticed that you tried," James said. They all looked at Jenna. She was wiping her eyes. The others around her were patting her on the back, but they were more talking to each other than interacting with her. "The others," James said. "Try to listen to one of the others."

Harper said, "Anyone in particular? They're all basically pod people."

Krista looked the table over, from end to end. "The one in the green shirt," she said.

Krista and James watched. The girl in the green shirt was whispering to another girl. The listening girl was laughing. She would lean forward every so often. They realized it was very regular intervals. "She's chanting," James said. "The girl in the green is chanting. I'm sure of it."

Harper took a deep breath. She'd been pulled in so quickly trying to hear Jenna's thoughts. But maybe it wouldn't be expecting this. Harper listened in to the green shirt's mind. She was expecting James to be right. She was expecting chanting. This was more like a stadium of people singing together. It wasn't in unison, but it wasn't chaotic either. It was more like an echo, or like you had two clips of the same video, just one starting slightly later than the other. Harper tried to make out the chant, but the echo made her feel dizzy any time she tried to focus. Harper pulled out when she felt Krista's hand on her own. Harper said, "You guys," but stopped when she saw their expressions.

Harper looked back at the table. While Jenna was getting her things together (and being so oblivious to everyone else that she had to be back to normal) all of her friends were staring at Harper. If she had snuck in, then she was busted now. "Okay," said Harper, "So what do we do here?"

"I've been considering wetting my pants," Krista said. "But I'm open to other suggestions."

"Jenna," James said. "We should do something for Jenna."

After a silence, Krista said, "James, when they eventually capture us, and they will, and when they ask whose brain they should eat first, and they will, I'm pointing directly to you, because you're obviously not using yours."

"Brent was very appreciative, and he remembered it on some level. Maybe if we display kindness, it will confuse the entity and undermine the depths and level of its control."

There was another silence, then Harper spoke. "Even if we agree with this idea in principle, how can we be kind to Jenna?"

"Maybe we can complement her looks?" James asked.

"Not without throwing up in my mouth a little," Krista said.

"Fine," James said. "I'll give her a compliment." He paused. "What should I tell her?"

Krista said, "Try telling her that she looks popular evil today instead of crazy evil like she has been."

"Maybe don't compliment her looks," Harper said. "Maybe try asking her why she was upset."

"No way," Krista said. "We can't ask her what's wrong with her today."

"Don't be petty." Harper said.

"No," Krista said. "Really. You think that if you go over and ask Jenna why she was just crying that she's going to see that as being nice? She'll think that you're looking for weaknesses."

"But this isn't Jenna under the entity's control anymore," James said.

"I know that, you dingbat," Krista said. "But she's still mean and sneaky and looks down on niceness."

James nodded. "She likes getting things, for sure. What do we have that she'd actually take?"

They were quiet again, and lunch was ending before long. "Do we have any candy?" James said.

Harper looked in her lunch bag. "I have a snack-size chocolate bar. I guess that's kind of sad."

"So is Jenna," Krista said, "It's perfect. Or at least it's what we have. Either way, I say go with it."

Harper handed it to James. He stared at it for a moment, and he said, "So I hand this to her and tell her that I hope it makes her day a little better?"

Krista opened her mouth, but when Harper shook her head, Krista said, "Yeah, that'll work."

James looked back down at the candy bar. "Well," he said, "I suppose that I should hand it off before the heat from my hands melts it." With that, James stood and went to Jenna's table. The whole time, all of Jenna's cronies stared at him James didn't flinch. In fact, he seemed unaware of any attention. He walked up to the group and held the mini candy out. "Jenna," he said, "I recognize that this candy is small, but I still hope that it gives you some degree of comfort or happiness."

Jenna stared at James. For a moment, James even thought that she might have appreciated it. But that stopped when Jenna said, "God, what is wrong with you?"

The whole table laughed. James pulled the candy back towards his body. Part of him wanted to use his powers to shove one of the kids into another, to have their heads knock together or their ankles twist. But he knew that he couldn't. Instead, he said, "Well, I'm glad I could make you laugh, anyway."

James turned and was walking away, but he still heard Jenna say, "Whatever, freak."

When James got back to the table, he tossed the candy in front of Harper. "I guess you can have it back."

"They were jerks," Harper said. It wasn't a question.

"To nobody's surprise," Krista said. After a pause she said, "You okay, James?"

James shrugged. "I got laughed at by popular kids. I believe that's a typical day."

Krista smiled. "James, you had a solid one-liner."

"Jenna couldn't tell," Harper said. "Don't you think that's odd?"

Krista said, "Like I said before, back to her usual, 'I don't care about others' self."

James shook his head. "Do you think that it's just her? Has anyone else in school acted or thought the way that she has?"

Harper looked around the lunch hall. "Let me listen," she said. She started with one of the lunch monitors. He was imagining taking one of the smartass tech ed kids into the bathroom and slamming the stall door on his head. Harper assumed that this was normal for him. Next, Harper tried listening to one of the AV kids. He was rehearsing an Oscar acceptance speech where he explained how his high school classmates were all insensitive duds. That was absolutely normal. Finally, Harper listened to one of the quiet kids. One of the boys that she only half recognized. What Harper heard made her gasp. She figured that the boy might be lonely or angry, but the scenes that he was narrating included burning people slowly,

69

cutting them to pieces to his chosen playlist, watching whole classes die from poison gas. It was like looking at one of those paintings of hell. Harper snapped out. "That boy. The one with the dark hair, orange t-shirt."

Krista spotted him before James. "The one by himself near the chip rack?"

"Yes," Harper said. "He's...well, he's wrong."

"Wrong?" James asked. "In what sense?"

"He's in a very bad place. Like, he has bad thoughts."

James frowned. "Do you think he's being controlled?"

Before Harper could answer, Krista said, "Oh, crap. Jenna's table." When Harper looked, she saw what Krista saw. The whole table was staring at the kid in the orange shirt. Then, like a wave, they turned one by one towards Harper, each with a little smirk on her face. "Does this mean he's being influenced?" Harper asked.

"No," James said. "It means two other things. First, it means that that boy is not under control, but they see him as an opportunity. The other thing is simpler; we need to be very careful going forward."

~ * ~

Sure enough, the rest of the day, Krista felt like she was being watched. Going through the halls, she felt like there were five sets of eyes on her at all times. In PE, she felt like the bleachers were full while she tried to just stay out of the way in volleyball. By the time that the final bell rang, she was glad to be able to just walk home. She headed towards the park so that she could get lost in some bushes and come out the other side invisible. There were a few kids playing there, but none of them were watching her. They were arguing, it looked like. It made Krista wonder how early kids started being jerks. Maybe the school wasn't the cause of everything. Maybe it was just the place where everyone's evil came out or got magnified.

When Krista came out of the bushes, she looked around carefully. There weren't any other high schoolers around. There were a couple of adults at the edge of the park, watching the kids. Krista took her time walking home, watching the town. She tried to think of who the kid with the orange shirt was. She thought that he was probably from her neighborhood. It would explain why he was so angry. But she couldn't place if he was a McKenzie, a Rausch, or maybe a Baker. But then it seemed like he should've been with his siblings. She tried to think if any of them had black sheep. Then again, in some families, it was hard to stand out as a black sheep.

As Krista cycled through their first names, she saw a little boy at the edge of his school's playground. He was standing very still and watching something. Krista walked closer slowly, making sure that she didn't step on anything loud that might give her away. She was still about fifty feet away when the boy pulled back his arm and threw a rock. It hit the ground, and a squirrel ran off. The kid threw a second rock, and that one missed, too. Krista shook her head. She looked at the ground around her. There was a fist sized red rock in the ground. She bent down to grab it. Maybe if she could hit the kid in the back or the elbow, it would scare the kid so much that he wouldn't do it again. Krista felt the weight of the rock in her hand, its roughness on her skin. She pictured the rock hitting the kid in the back of the head. Pictured the lump that would show up in just a few seconds. Instead of throwing it, though, she let it drop to the ground.

It would be nice if it was as easy as picking off one kid with a little rock, but Krista knew better. This kid would be pissed off, then he'd do something worse to some other animal. Or to a sibling. The rock would make her feel better, and that would be it. And that wasn't enough.

The kid picked up another rock, but he just tossed it a few inches up in the air, then caught it. He kept tossing it as he walked off, dropping it now and then. Krista went pretty much straight home after that. A few blocks from home, she went down an alley and let herself become visible again. The walk definitely hadn't made her feel any better. It hadn't exactly made her feel worse, either.

Krista went into her house and looked around. She went over to her mom's room and peeked in. She wasn't there. Krista decided to look in her room. When she got there, it was still empty, but she felt like she'd felt after lunch. Like someone was watching. Krista went to the kitchen. The feeling went away a little, but not entirely. She decided that she'd do her homework at the kitchen table. She took out her math textbook and her worksheet, and she tried not to think about how she'd sleep tonight. She tried to just work through the problems.

~ * ~

James had a hard time distinguishing between actual threats and what he simply noticed as a potential threat simply because he was looking. There was a fellow student in the hall that said, "Watch it, freak," even though he'd been the one to collide with James. In Biology, what should have been a simple dissection was distracting because everyone in the room had a sharp object. Just focusing was difficult.

By the end of the day, James was exhausted. He fully recognized that he wasn't thinking logically or practically. And yet, he couldn't shut down. Any kind of episode would only increase his vulnerability. James needed to clear his head, reduce the stimuli without becoming totally unaware of his surroundings. He started tapping his fingers on the side of his ribs, playing out a steady beat. It was a good start towards calming him.

As he walked towards his locker at the final bell, he could feel his anxiety decreasing a bit. The regular bumps and prods in the hallway were minor agitations and not full-blown crises. When he got to his locker, though, some of the girls from Jenna's table were there, clearly waiting for him. James considered simply walking past his locker. He was in no state to deal with these girls, and he could access most of his homework at home, making up the balance before school tomorrow. He knew, though, that this solution was impractical. While he might be able to take care of the homework, the girls would almost certainly follow him. This could become a significant problem if one of his parents saw it. How could James possibly explain their presence in a convincing way? In addition, confronting this problem head on (like the peaches, but on a more severe scale) might provide him with yet another opportunity to observe them interacting.

James maintained his tapping and approached them. "Excuse me," he said, "but that's my locker."

"Nobody owns the lockers, stupid," one of the girls said.

James slowed his tapping, but he kept the basic rhythm. "The school does," he said.

The girls looked at each other, then laughed. "Why are you so weird?" a second girl asked.

James was struck by the fact that this could be simple teenage cruelty. But if it wasn't the entity, then why were they at his locker in the first place? Was it just kind of residual animosity from the incident at lunch?

"God," one of the girls said, "look at him just staring." They laughed again.

James looked at the floor. "Where's Jenna?" he asked.

One of the girls laughed. "I think the weirdo has a crush on Jenna."

Most of the others laughed, but one of them made a face. "Gross," she said.

James kept tapping out a beat. "Where's Jenna?" he asked again.

The girls stopped laughing. James thought that one of them (the one that had characterized his interest in Jenna as "gross") started to look a bit wobbly, like she might faint. The girl who had accused James of being interested in Jenna said, "She wouldn't want to talk to you anyway, freak."

"Probably not," James admitted. "I was just expressing concern because she seemed so upset, but you probably wouldn't be at liberty to discuss her troubles with me anyway."

"Why do you talk like that?" the ringleader asked.

"I can't imagine that you really want me to answer that." James was feeling surprisingly calm and confident, and the girls were appearing to lose interest.

"What?" one of the girls asked. Another was staring at the floor. James looked at the spot on the floor she was looking at. It didn't seem particularly noteworthy.

"Look," a third said, "we know you can't stop being a freak, but at least stay away from Jenna. That's all we're saying."

James nodded. "In that case, perhaps you could move so that I can access my locker?"

"Let's go," one of the girls said. A couple of the others nodded. The one who had been staring at the floor shook her head a little, then she rubbed her eyes. The ringleader shot the other girl a dirty look, "Okay,

James," the ringleader said. "We'll let you get your books and crap, but stay away from Jenna or we'll tell the principal you're stalking her."

It was a much milder threat than James expected. Maybe they didn't want to get caught threatening him. "Duly noted," James said. "See you at lunch tomorrow?"

The ringleader rolled her eyes and walked off. The others followed, but not in unison. James was surprised that they moved at different paces. He watched them walk off before going to his locker. He stopped tapping as he opened the locker, but, by that time, he was sufficiently relaxed anyway. It had been a strange interaction. It seemed like they'd been waiting to intimidate him, but their parting shot had been a weak one. He wished Harper had been there to get a read on their thoughts. He'd have to review their words and actions. If nothing else, he'd have something to discuss at lunch tomorrow.

~ * ~

Harper was listening to different snatches of thought as she walked through the hall. So many of the other students felt fear and frustration. From their dating prospects, to their home lives, to upcoming tests, she wondered why there weren't *more* people like the boy in the orange shirt. The scariest part of it all was that all this anxiety just seemed to be normal. Nobody seemed all that worried about the fact that they were worried. In fact, there were a bunch of people putting up superhero decorations for homecoming while worrying about pimples or getting yelled at by parents.

Eventually, Harper did pass Brent. He must have been coming back from PE and into the main bank of classrooms. Harper kept some distance, but she started listening in. It was noisy in his head, but not quite like before. This wasn't a chant, and Harper didn't feel herself getting sucked in. Instead, it almost felt like she was listening to Brent talk to himself, like a person might if they were trying to remember something.

Harper watched Brent move. If all the noise in his head bothered him, he certainly didn't show it. He kept up his slow amble. Every now and then he'd check out some girl or shake his head at some nerd, but he mostly just kept moving, totally separate from any of the people around him even while he was right in the middle of all of them. Harper wondered if that was why the thing targeted people like Jenna and Brent. Maybe they'd built up walls around themselves to the point that no one would notice if they weren't in control of things anymore. Maybe they didn't have enough personality or interest to make themselves hard to erase. Maybe she was just being petty. Harper told herself to remember to ask James and Krista about it later.

Before tuning out of Brent's mind, Harper gave it one last try. She tried to catch some kind of pattern, even if it was just a different kind of chant. After a few seconds, she realized that it couldn't be just Brent talking to himself. What Harper realized was that there was more than one voice talking. In fact, she started to catch a number of voices chattering to each other. She tried to separate them out, to listen to just one, but she couldn't. It would've been like trying to grab just one drop of water. But still, she could sense a deep voice under all the others. It was the strongest, but more than that. If all the others were the water in the pool, then this one was the paint on the bottom of the pool, setting the color of the water. It was angry and commanding. Harper pulled back out of Brent's head. She slowed down a little and watched Brent walk away, just looking around. He seemed not to have a care in the world.

Harper felt tired then. She thought about going to the nurse and telling her she didn't feel well. The nurse almost never doubted her complaints of feeling sick. But there would probably be a phone call home and a slew of questions from her mother. Better to make it to class and zone out, trying to not be noticed. She went to the side of the hall, resting one hand on the wall whenever possible. She was actually doing pretty well until she saw the group of girls from Jenna's table. They were watching her and laughing to each other. That wasn't necessarily surprising, and they weren't even threatening her, but she found herself hating them to an irrational degree. The reasonable part of her mind told the hating part that it made no sense to take it personally. That they were just heartless and cruel and they might not even be in control of their behavior. But it didn't really help to calm her down. She still hated their faces.

Harper closed her eyes and leaned against the wall. It was hard, recognizing that she was angry, not being able to get rid of the anger and having this washed out feeling on top of everything. When she opened her eyes and looked back where the girls had been, Harper saw that they were gone, but it didn't make her feel any better. Instead, she just felt angry.

Ella, had stopped to look at Harper. When Harper looked at her, Ella put her hand on Harper's elbow. "You okay?" she asked.

Harper said, "Oh yeah, just perfect." When Ella's smile faded, Harper said, "Keep going".

Ella backed up. She said, "I just wanted to see…"

Harper cocked her head and narrowed her eyes. Ella stepped back, then she walked away. Harper opened her mouth to yell, but then something shifted in her head. Harper put her left hand over her mouth. Poor Ella really had just been checking on her. After a few seconds, Harper shook her head and did her best to move without falling over.

She got to her class and dropped her books on her desk. She could feel people looking at her. She didn't need her powers to figure out why. It was all she could do to sit in her desk and take out a pencil without screaming at everyone. As she looked at the board, Harper tried to slow her breathing down and relax. On the board was a series of dates related to the Civil War. As Harper copied the dates down, she realized that she had not actually been safe from Brent's influence. She hadn't been sucked in as quickly, fully, or strongly as she had been with Jenna, but it was obvious once she thought about it. She'd tried to take a dip in the pool, now she felt the rage and anxiety. And, worse, she'd been mean to Ella for no good reason.

By the end of class, Harper was back to normal. She still felt tired, but even that wasn't entirely bad. The tired feeling kept the strongest feelings of anger at bay. Harper looked around at her classmates. They all looked so bored. It struck her that all the teachers and parents and other adults must have no clue what was going on in their heads. Instead of recognizing the panic and anger going on inside the students the adults must see nothing but lifeless sacks of sarcasm and emojis. It left Harper very depressed.

~ * ~

The three of them met in the morning. They didn't have to call each other or anything. They all knew.

"Well," James said. "Let's compare notes, but quickly," They each took a turn relating what had happened. After they all finished, James said, "Be careful. It's had time to plot against us.

"Do we know that we're a real or primary target of the plot?" Krista said.

"Not going to lie," Harper said, "I'm a little surprised that you're trying to be the voice of reason here."

Krista rolled her eyes. "Listen, dork," she said, "I just meant that we should focus on what we need to focus on. Like, do we mainly need to watch out for other people like orange shirt, you know?"

James rubbed his left ear. "I do get it. Yes, you might be right."

Krista smirked. "Why thank you, James. I appreciate your vote of confidence."

James nodded. "I'm going to ignore the strong possibility that your statement is largely sarcasm and try to focus on our main goal today, which is finding the fellow in the orange shirt."

"Have we figured out who he is?" Harper asked.

"I was trying to figure out what family he's from," Krista said, "but I couldn't place him."

"If nothing else, we'll see him at lunch," James said. "Harper, if you see him, see if you can listen in again. If your sense of the voice is correct, then maybe you could pick up on some shift in tone or rhythm between yesterday's thoughts and today's."

"But don't get sucked in," Krista said. "That's the last thing we need."

Harper said, "So I need to be on the lookout for a boy I don't really know and who I remember mostly from clothes that he won't be wearing today and I should be trying to listen to his mind in careful detail while not letting myself get too sucked in. Got it."

"It's not like today will be simple for any of us, Harper." James said.

Harper sighed. "I know. It's just, do you guys ever wish we could switch powers?"

"We did combine them before," James said. "Perhaps we should again?"

"That's not what I mean," said Harper. "I mean actually switching for a while."

"If you want to have a pity party, keep in mind that I have the most useless power right now," Krista said.

"That's not true," James said. "You were able to get into the locker room of the football team at half-time. Not only is that impressive, but it also did yield some valuable intelligence."

"Intelligence from a football locker room," Krista said. "How's that for irony?"

"Plus," Harper said, "I can hear things, but I can't really do anything, you know?"

"Well," James said, "I can do things, but I still can't really do anything in a very real sense."

Krista squinted at him. "Sometimes the more that I talk to you, the less I understand you."

"I get it," Harper said. "I guess none of us are really doing anything. I mean, have we actually done anything to whatever this is yet?"

"I think we've pissed it off," Krista said. "But I don't know if that's helpful,"

"It is, in the sense that it helps us to see it be active, and that helps us study it," James said.

Krista patted James on the shoulder, "Leave it to you to find something good in our coming deaths."

"I don't let most people make physical contact with me," James said.

"Okay," Harper said. "I guess this is going to have to take the place of an actual pep talk,"

Both Krista and James said, "Sorry."

Harper laughed a little. "Well, that's a little better, anyway."

The three of them parted ways. Krista looked to each side as she went to her locker. It was hard to determine what she should be watching for. The weirdo in the orange shirt, the girls at Jenna's table, Jenna again. By the time that she got to her locker, Krista felt creeped out. She was surprised then, when there were some boys around her locker. At first, she felt like turning around. Teenage boys were a menace individually, so three of them together was basically a horror movie.

She paused for a moment and realized that they weren't waiting for her. They were looking at one of those stupid flyers that was advertising one of the upcoming dances. It was of Batman and Catwoman dancing. The boys were laughing about something (probably about how dumb the dance was going to be) and didn't seem to notice her at all. Krista went to her locker, keeping an eye on the boys. As she put most of her books in her locker, taking out only her math things, she noticed one of the boys had looked over at her. Krista kept unloading her things, pretending not to notice. She could feel her heartbeat picking up. When she closed her locker and turned, she saw that the boy was looking back at her. He smiled at her and nodded.

At first, Krista froze a little. She tried not to let her eyes get too big. She nodded back and walked off, making sure that she didn't turn back to see whether or not the boy was still looking at her. The boy wasn't bad looking, actually. Not dreamy or anything, but above average. But during a feud with some horrible force possessing the school probably wasn't the best time to start dating. Then again, if Krista waited for a normal stretch of life, she'd be single forever. Like her mother was now.

~ * ~

James often had difficulty in English class. While the spelling and grammar portions were never a problem, the abstractions of interpretation often challenged him. Today they were discussing the *Odyssey*. While he was able to track the elements of the hero's journey (a simple checklist, really, not particularly complex) the discussion of what the suitors meant was less clear.

He looked around the room. There were a couple of other people who were at least trying to take notes, but many were just staring off into space. Even worse, it was clear that a number of his classmates were simply doodling, perhaps not even listening at all (though, at the beginning of the year, two different teachers had announced that it was acceptable for students to doodle in class if it helped them to pay attention, which James remembered, because he felt that type of accommodation was not comparable to one that he or Harper or Krista deserved). It made James realize that the teachers must also sometimes fall prey to the entity running the school. While the teachers were free from the hormonal issues that the students dealt with, they would have a steady level of frustration, always being ignored, disrespected or otherwise annoyed by the student body; they must have a low level of anger that would make them just as interesting to dominate as many of the students were.

James came out of his thoughts and realized that the teacher had asked a question. While James didn't always answer the questions in English classes, he would often reinterpret. Not only did it improve his grade, it also made class function more smoothly and efficiently. Right now, he realized that he was just like all of his classmates: lost without context and waiting for someone else to take care of the problem. He watched his teacher's face, something he often didn't do. He wished he'd been paying attention. There was a look that even James could recognize as exasperation. She sighed and said, "While true love would have meant something different to the Greeks than it does to us, there were still practical concerns of patrilineal power. Also, Penelope shows herself to be Odysseus's intellectual equal by outwitting the suitors."

Mrs. Benson turned back to the board, where she wrote down a few more key terms related to Greek culture, talking as she went. After she'd written down the terms and given some explanation, she played a video for them. It was of a middle-aged man with a beard discussing the structures of Greek heroes and epics. Every now and then, they would play simulations of Greek warriors fighting. Somehow, the class seemed even less engaged in the video than they had been in class lecture. In all fairness, it wasn't an engaging video.

After the video ended, the teacher asked the class how the video added to their discussion. When the class was silent, she said, "For instance, do we see Odysseus as influencing some of the heroes that we see in today's books and movies?"

Mainly out of a sense of sympathy, James said, "Many heroes in books and movies do seem to experience a sense of isolation, fighting against some larger system."

The teacher looked at him. James could not entirely make out what her expression meant. "I suppose that's true, James. Can you think of a particular example?"

James now regretted answering. Whatever his response was, it was likely to result in ridicule from his classmates later in the day. James said, "Batman?"

There were a couple of chuckles, but the teacher was able to frown them into silence. "Actually," the teacher said, "there are a number of ways in which Batman can fit into the category of an epic hero." She went on to discuss the significance of Bruce Wayne's parents having been murdered. James was surprised at how much she seemed to know about Batman. It made him wonder if Mrs. Benson might have had a hand in selecting the homecoming theme.

The rest of the class went in a fairly typical fashion. Near the end, something light pelted James in the back of the head. He looked down at the floor. There was a little folded triangle of paper. Someone had drawn a bat signal on the side. James decided to not pay any more attention to it during class, but, when class ended, he picked it up as he gathered his things. On his way to his locker, James unfolded it. There was a series of drawings of him and the teacher. If he were to show it to a teacher or principal, he likely could have a complaint of harassment. But that would lead to a long and quite possibly fruitless investigation to see who had done the drawings.

So, instead of turning it in, James tore it into pieces and tossed the pieces into a few different trash cans in the hall, trying to make sure that they couldn't be put back together. James was just tossing away the last scraps of the drawing when he saw the student who had been wearing the orange shirt and thinking horrible thoughts yesterday. James froze when he saw him, and the boy seemed to recognize that James was staring. James nodded and walked away. He suspected that the boy was following him. James wanted to keep from panicking. He had to. So he tried to focus on the empty space behind him, giving a light push that would work as a kind of shield. He slowed down a bit and focused as hard as he could. He could feel the boy getting closer, and then he felt the boy stop. It was a strange feeling, not like someone touching his skin, but also not like a breeze or a source of heat diffused in a room. James could actually feel the contact, even if he wasn't fully capable of processing its specific sensation. That was fine with James. He heard the boy mutter, "The hell?" and he felt the contact end. After a few seconds (just to ensure safety) James let his shield deteriorate. It had actually worked.

~ * ~

At lunch, James found himself struggling to effectively articulate the significance of his discovery. Krista seemed to be genuinely trying to be supportive. "James," she said, "if we end up getting in a fight, and we're bound to, eventually, you'll be, like, invulnerable."

James looked down, trying to find a way to explain while maintaining the tone that his mother would refer to as "diplomatic." "I appreciate the fact that you're trying to validate my discovery," he began, "but I suspect that the deeper implications of this discovery move far beyond the narrow world of fistfights and hallway wrestling matches."

Krista got a look on her face that James couldn't fully describe, but that he could easily identify as a sign that ridicule was coming shortly.

"Okay," she said, "then please enlighten the dullards about its subtle complexities."

"Well," James said, "I certainly didn't mean to imply that I have a monopoly of wisdom."

"James," Harper said, "this might be one of those times when apologizing just ends up doing more harm than good. You can probably jump to the explanation."

James felt a greater level of panic than he had when the orange-shirted student had been following him. "Listen," he said, "I understand that we have a natural sense of panic. There's still a lot that we don't know. But part of the point of my breakthrough is that it is, in fact, a genuine breakthrough."

Krista nodded, then said, "I'm not sure that this helps with the whole 'arrogant' thing."

James could feel the pressure of his own anger forcing him down.

He felt the process of his explanation breaking down in the face of Krista's seemingly willful stupidity. He heard Harper telling Krista to lay off, to give James another chance to say what he meant. And, on some level, he experienced a feeling of gratitude. But he still felt fundamentally interrupted. Closed in. He took a deep breath. "Listen," he said, "we're still learning, but that means that our greatest displays of power could be ahead of us. Think about it. Our bodies are still changing…"

"Oh my God, James," Krista said, "I already sat through this in health class."

James crossed his arms. "Joke if you must, but think about what this implies."

Krista and Harper looked at each other. Before either one could really reply, though, the yelling began. At first, James thought that perhaps he was the cause of it. After being able to raise a shield, perhaps he would also be able to force people into agitation and action. But as James crept out of himself, he recognized that something else was causing it.

The three of them together looked to the table across from them. It had a group of students who were usually quiet. Today, three of them were screaming amongst each other. The nature of the disagreement was unclear, but it was clear that they were angry and that things were escalating quickly.

"This isn't good," Krista said.

The statement was stupid, of course, and James thought about calling her out on this stupidity, getting back at her for needling at him. But the counterproductive nature of this was even clearer as the students at the table stood up. Krista moved towards and in front of Harper, and James recognized it as not a movement of fear but instead of protecting the most physically vulnerable member of the group. James tried to follow suit, imagining another shield, but the movement among the students at the next table was so erratic that he couldn't visualize how it would be effective. He looked at the other tables. Students seemed to be more captivated than worried.

One of the people from the table let loose a string of obscenities, and then he stormed off, heading towards the three's table. James tried to focus on the boy's ankles, hoping to trip him, keep him from getting too close, but the boy was moving too quickly, and the noise was too agitating, keeping James from being able to focus to the extent that he should. To James's surprise, the boy passed the table without incident. James relaxed, but only slightly. The noise was still severe and unrelenting.

Even beneath the noise, James heard Harper gasp. The boy had turned and screamed a few more obscenities. As he did so, he walked back towards his table, stopping right behind the three's table. After he finished yelling, he looked down at Harper and said, "What the hell are you looking at?"

Before any of them could react, the boy reached back and punched Harper in the face. Krista rose and charged at the boy. James was surprised by how quickly she moved, and the boy seemed very surprised, too. He hadn't even pulled back for a second punch and Krista had kneed him in the groin. The boy doubled over and Krista brought her forearm down hard over the back of the boy's neck. He dropped to the floor. James looked over at the table where the yelling had started. Two of the other boys were heading over. Mercifully, one of the lunchroom monitors blew their whistle. Krista didn't look up and James wondered if she was just pretending or if she truly hadn't heard. It didn't seem likely that she could have totally missed it, but it was hard to say for sure.

The boys now seemed to be in a trance as the lunch monitors came over. They told the two boys at the table to go to the office. As the boys left, one monitor spoke into a walkie-talkie while the other came over to the table and grabbed Krista by the arm. "Okay," she said, "Let's go."

Krista made no attempt to resist, but as she was being led off, she looked directly at James and said, "Keep her safe, James. It's up to you to keep her safe."

James looked down at Harper. Her nose was bleeding, and she was crying. James got out of his seat. The lunch monitor had finished on the walkie talkie and was asking Harper if she was okay. The question was absurd, of course. James knelt down by Harper, but he was unsure of what else to do. He could try to sit her up so that he could rub her back, but that would likely make her nose bleed even harder, and he wasn't really sure that rubbing her back would actually be that comforting for Harper. It rarely made James feel better. Instead, he simply took her hand in his and said,

"I'm here, Harper."

Harper squeezed his hand back. "God," she said, "oh, God."

They stayed that way until the monitor separated them, taking Harper to the nurse's office. James thought of what Krista said. "I want to come with her," he told the monitor.

The monitor looked at James. He couldn't quite read her face. It may have been some weird combination of sympathy and worry. Or maybe she was just losing patience after the fight. Whatever her feelings were, her response to James's request was, "Sorry, but you can't come with your girlfriend."

And so James watched Harper get led off, still crying. He was terrified. He wouldn't really know what was happening with either Harper or Krista, and they wouldn't be there for him, to watch his back. James felt like looking around the lunch hall, catching what threats were present, what horrible things might be coming for him. But he also didn't feel like looking around, didn't want all the eyes to be turned upon him, radiating that sense of danger back upon him. He couldn't look. In the end he couldn't do it.

~ * ~

Harper sat in the principal's office, holding an ice pack to her nose with her left hand. She watched people come in and out. Krista had been brought in while Harper was with the nurse, but when she came out of the principal's inner office, she looked Harper right in the eye. Krista didn't say anything, so Harper listened to her thoughts. She gave two: "Get home" and "stay safe." Harper nodded, and Krista looked away as she was led off. Harper wondered how bad of punishment Krista had gotten.

A few seconds later, the principal came out of his office. He stood in front of Harper, not saying anything. Then he sighed and said, "Are you okay to talk, or do you need to lie down?"

Instead of answering, Harper stood up. She did it slowly, and she let herself wobble a little when she was fully upright. The principal steadied her by her elbow. Harper let herself listen to his thoughts for a second, just trying to sense what he knew and what he'd ask. His thoughts were panicked, but that was no surprise. He also didn't seem to present a real threat to Harper. His main thoughts were about lawyers and the local newspaper. On some level, Harper realized that this could give her an advantage to work with, but she also remembered Krista's message, and she didn't feel like talking to the principal any more than she had to.

So, after giving the principal a little nod of appreciation for the help in balancing, Harper said, "I'll be fine, really. It was just all so shocking."

The principal started to lead her into his inner office, but he still watched her carefully, like she was a balloon that might either pop or blow away. "Shocking," he said, "is exactly how I'd put it."

After the principal got Harper safely to her seat, he went around his desk and sat in his own chair. The chair looked old, and it creaked a little when he sat down. Harper wondered how many different principals the chair had outlasted. "The main thing that I want to see," he said, "is how you're doing after all this."

Harper shrugged. It was a ridiculous question, but given what she heard of his thoughts, she could understand what the principal was really asking. "I think I'll be okay. Physically, I mean." She watched the principal's body language. He was leaning back in his chair, but he didn't really look relaxed. It was more like he was just trying to lean away from the unpleasant situation, to keep a barrier of safety.

"You're worried about what might happen in the coming days," he said.

"If Krista hadn't stepped in, who knows what would've happened." Harper was quiet while she listened to his thoughts. He was wondering if he'd been too hard on Krista, but Harper wasn't able to catch what punishment he'd given her. "I just want to feel safe."

The principal's expression softened a little. "Look," he said, "there is absolutely nothing more important to me than the safety of my students. And that's for every single one of you guys."

Harper's nose still throbbed. "I appreciate that," she said, "I really do." She hoped she didn't sound too sarcastic.

"Of course," the principal said, "Edward might not feel very safe tomorrow, given what your friend did."

Harper wished that she had James's power. She'd use it to tip the principal's chair back. "Edward," she said. "That's the name of the kid that punched me in the face."

"That's the name of the boy that your friend beat to the ground."

Harper tried to slow her breathing. She couldn't let herself get into an argument with the principal. "Krista has never been violent before today," Harper said. "Not once, and the only reason that she did anything today was to protect me."

Harper listened into the principal's thoughts. He was still thinking about lawyers, but now also about parents. And he was thinking that he hated Harper for defending Krista. "I hope that's true," the principal said. "While it's true that she has not been violent, many teachers find her unmotivated and disrespectful."

Harper had to stifle a laugh. He wasn't lying. "If you kicked out all of the kids who were lazy or rude, I can't imagine that there would be many of us left."

The principal chuckled. "You have a point there. And, for the record, I'm not looking to expel anyone. Let's get to what we need to get to, here. Can you give me your version of what happened?"

Harper lowered the ice pack. Her face still hurt, but at least the bleeding had stopped.

"First, there was some yelling at the boys' table. I'm not even sure what it was about. They were just screaming like maniacs, cursing and everything." Harper paused. She made herself look upset while she listened to the principal's thoughts. He was considering whether or not Harper and Krista could have had a chance to make sure that their stories overlapped. He seemed to expect that they wouldn't have had the chance. Harper pushed on. "So then the one kid, Edward, I guess, started to storm off. But then he came back, and well, it was hard to register everything that happened. He yelled again, and he was glaring at me, and he just started punching me." This time, Harper didn't have to pretend to be upset.

Harper looked at the floor, but she listened to the principal's thoughts. There were two strands of thoughts going on. The louder of the two was that Harper's story matched Krista's enough that it must be the truth. The other was a quiet but steady complaint about the students and parents that he had to deal with. "Well, I'll be having a good long talk with the boys and their parents, and I think that you should feel safe. Now, your mother's been called, and I'll talk to your teachers about why you're having to go home early. Rest for the rest of the day, and come back feeling safe."

"Thanks," Harper said. She wasn't entirely sure she was supposed to get up and go or if she waited for the principal to excuse her. She realized that she'd never been sent to the principal's office before. She'd been in the main office for IEP meetings, but that was always with a large crowd, and she generally wanted to get out as quickly as possible. Now, she watched her principal stare back at her, wondering what was going to happen next. He eventually picked up a pencil and rotated it between his fingers. "So," he said, "if there's nothing else."

Harper nodded, then she stopped. "Actually," she said, "I'd like to hear what the boys' version of events was. Why did they do it? Why did they come after me?"

The principal stopped rotating the pencil. He started telling her how it would be unethical to give details to Harper, just as Harper would not want him running back to the boys and telling them what she said. She zoned out from what he was saying and listened to his thoughts. The two strands were still there, but the quieter one had become too hard to decipher. She could only sense that it was there. The louder strand was expressing uncertainty. He was thinking about the fact that the boys had no sense of why they'd done what they'd done. They didn't seem to understand their own actions, and that scared him. Harper could understand. After the principal finished his sermon, Harper said, "I understand."

He stared at Harper, and she quickly pulled out of his mind. Even if the principal was mostly laughable, whatever was producing the second thread could be part of the danger and she didn't want to get sucked in. "Can I wait in the nurse's office until my mom gets here?"

The principal nodded, probably relieved. "That's a good idea. Do you want someone to get your things for you? I could have one of the aides do it if you wanted to give us your key."

Harper thought for a bit about that. "Maybe we could have an aide help me to my locker?"

The principal raised his eyebrows. "Is it a good idea for you to be walking around?"

Harper said, "I'm fine, really. It's just easier for me to look and see what I need than it is for me to try and remember what's where in my locker."

The principal nodded slowly. Maybe he was wondering if Harper was hiding something in her locker that she wouldn't want an aide to find. If that was the case, then it apparently wasn't a huge concern for him, because he said, "As long as you feel safe, I'm happy to send someone with you."

"Thank you," Harper said. He nodded again and picked up his phone. He asked his secretary to call down Tachick, an aide that Harper recognized as having the ability to recognize what the minimum level of effort would be in any situation. On a day like today, that was exactly what Harper would hope for. Hopefully, James's day was settling down equally well.

~ * ~

James was not able to focus during History. Instead of taking notes on the military strategies of the American Revolution, James was putting things into two categories: things he currently knew and things he still needed to discover (this positive phrasing was something his father had suggested.) He knew that he would likely regret this later, during an exam or paper, but he felt that taking poor, distracted notes would be less helpful to him than writing the list would be.

Under the "currently know" heading, he had been able to produce a number of items. A chant exists. The entity had left Jenna. The entity was able to inhabit multiple people at once. It preferred popular students. The boy in the orange shirt was not popular, but he still seemed to be of interest to the entity. His "Need to Discover" list had a number of items as well, but they all led back to the first item he'd written: how to defeat the entity.

He stared at it for a few seconds, then he added, "Where Harper is" and "Where Krista is" to the "Need" category. At first, this increased his anxiety. Of course, he knew that he couldn't say where they were, but seeing it down on paper, there in his own handwriting, made their absence more concrete. But after a deep breath and some tapping on his notebook, the heading of the second category did have the desired effect. While he didn't know their current whereabouts, the chances that he would go several days without seeing them was negligible. Beyond that, framing the issues as one of "needing to find" the information helped to suggest a path of action. While James did not imagine that a direct phone call to Krista's house would be advisable, texting Harper after school would be reasonable, and, given the nature of Harper's powers, it was absolutely reasonable to consider it likely that Harper would have read Krista's thoughts to know where she was. James looked at his list and tapped on his notebook. It made him feel better. Unfortunately, this was disrupted when the boy behind him leaned over and whispered to James, "Hey, freak, this is History, not band. Stop drumming."

James did indeed stop. This meant that the list not only failed to calm him but James also had no hope of calming down after being called out by a classmate. It was extraordinarily frustrating to recognize how quickly things could change. To add to his frustration, James could hear giggling behind him, giggling aimed at him, no doubt. He considered writing "why they're laughing" on his "need" list, but he ultimately decided against it. Although it was agitating, he didn't really need to know the reason.

Instead, James decided to focus on the lecture. Perhaps he still could get some level of focus and retain something from the day's lesson. The teacher was discussing the shift from conventional warfare to attempting surprise attacks. James knew that he should pay attention, not just for purposes of academic performance, but also because it might have some impact on his current situation. Still, he could not bring himself to catch all of the details.

The laughter came again, and it was hard to resist the temptation to turn around. James found it particularly troubling, because the teacher made no effort to challenge or even acknowledge the laughter. At least, she should have asked for quiet from the class. Instead, she simply droned on about how clever the revolutionaries were. It made James sympathize with the question of why they should be forced to learn this material, a question typically associated with laziness.

After yet another burst of laughter, James decided to start focusing on the back part of the underpants waistband of the boy behind him. James thought of the many times he had been "wedgied" as a younger child, and he visualized a slow but steady pull on the boy's waistband. Sure enough, there was a quiet groan and a bit of shifting from the seat behind James. James allowed himself a small smile, and he continued his steady pull on the waistband. The boy said "Hey," and then he stood up and said, "What the hell?" He turned around and looked at the boy behind him. "Dude," he said, and he pushed the boy with one hand while picking at his wedgie with the other. The whole class laughed, and the teacher finally noticed.

She did not, however, directly address the wedgie victim. Instead, she looked directly at James and said, "You all need to stop disrupting class, or I will have to punish you."

James felt a cold panic rising. He wasn't sure if it would be better to sit quietly, not engaging, or if it would be better to apologize. The boy behind him said, "This jackoff just grabbed my underwear. He should be kicked out of class."

The boy being accused said, "No I didn't. Why would I touch your nasty underwear?"

Before things could escalate, and without looking away from James, the teacher said, "I have asked that we not disrupt class, and it will not be disrupted any further than it already has been. Do we all understand my request?"

James wanted to look around. Surely some of his classmates would recognize that this was not the usual mode of speech for their teacher. But nobody spoke up. Instead, after a bit of grumbling, the boy behind James sat down, and the rest of class went back to their typical stupor. James sat, feeling intense anxiety and uncertain of what to do, for the rest of the class. When the bell rang, the teacher said, "I'll see you all tomorrow, when you will behave for the entirety of the class." This time, she didn't even need to look at James.

~ * ~

Krista had planned to take the long way home. Who knew when her mom would be home, but if Krista got home too early, then she could get busted. If she got home too late, then she might not be able to delete the voicemail that the school was sure to have left (finally, there was an upside to having a parent so poor that she still had a house phone).

So Krista wandered a little after she left the school. After she dropped out of sight, she found a tree to stand under. After a quick look around, she went invisible, and she set off again, being careful not to shake the tree branches as she went. It was getting cold, so she didn't want to stay outside for too long, but she also knew that going inside somewhere would probably mean becoming visible again (too many echoes, door creaks and other noises that she might not catch to try to stay invisible when inside).

Krista decided that she'd wander around the park a little and then go back to visible and browse the grocery store. If she ran into someone there and they asked why she wasn't in school, then she'd just pretend not to hear. Krista started towards the park, being careful to steer clear of any people or potential sources of noise. There was a little breeze, and with how cold the day was, Krista felt herself shivering, she hoped her teeth didn't start chattering.

She wondered how James was coping with being alone. In some ways, he seemed to be the best suited of the three of them for solitary work. But they'd come to rely on each other so much, especially lately, that it was hard to imagine making it through the day without some kind of help or just a check in from James or Harper. That made Krista worry about Harper too. Would Harper's mom let her go back to school right away? Krista didn't know how sane, normal parents made those kinds of decisions. She wondered if she should have thought "call me" to Harper when she saw her in the principal's office. It was hard to think straight in there.

Krista tucked her hands in her pockets. She needed to turn visible and get inside. The grocery store was a few blocks away, still. She'd need to get close, cut through an alley, and turn visible. She picked up her pace and headed in a straighter line for the store. She was about halfway there with a dog turned the corner and started walking toward her. She always hated that; the dogs could smell her or hear her or something, and they got confused. Sure enough, about twenty feet away, the dog stopped walking. Krista had pressed herself against the side of a building as tight as she could. She stayed still, but the dog was still definitely staring in her direction. When the dog refused to move, its owner shook the leash a couple of times. All the dog did was start barking. It would take a couple of slow steps towards Krista, then it would bark, and then it would back up again. Its tail was wagging, but the dog did not seem happy.

The dog's owner yelled something, then he tugged on the dog's leash again. The dog took a couple of steps forward, but it also started straining towards Krista. She tried her best to not move. The owner was trying to pull the dog along and that helped, but the dog seemed pretty determined to figure out what was going on. As they passed, the dog sniffed at her knees, and then barked loudly. The owner yelled at the dog and kept going. He looked in Krista's general direction, too, but then he shook his head and kept going. The dog barked the whole time.

After the dog and owner had gone, Krista hurried into the next alley. When she got halfway down the alley, Krista sat down, then did something she almost never let herself do: she cried. And hard. She didn't know how long she sat there for, but by the time she pulled herself together and was wiping her eyes, she felt cold and numb in just about every possible way. But even that felt good.

Krista stood up. She put a finger to her nose, closing one nostril, and she blew hard out of the other. As Krista wiped her nose on her jacket sleeve, she looked up and down the alley. The coast looked clear, so she turned visible and walked out of the alley, the opposite of the side she'd come in. There would still be a while before she could go home, but at least the store was in sight now. Krista wished that she had a mirror so that she could see if she looked crazy or just like a mess. Then she laughed at herself. The invisible girl who wanted to be able to see herself in the mirror.

She made it to the store and through the store without any trouble. A few "shouldn't you be in school" looks from store workers and customers, but no direct questions. Maybe her crazy look paid off. Or maybe they knew Krista's mother and just felt sorry for her. Either way, Krista would take this different kind of invisibility. After she warmed up from being in the store, she headed out again and made her way home. She was probably still a little early, but she decided to chance it. Krista took a deep breath, then she let herself in.

Krista opened the door, went in, and shut it, all as quickly as she could. She said, "Mom?" softly once, and then louder. There was no answer either time. Krista locked the door behind her. That would slow her mother down a bit if she did come home. Next, she went to the phone. There was only one message. It was exactly what she expected. "Your daughter was in a fight... sent home early... detention next week." Krista erased it. She was sure that she could forge a signature if they sent a note home, and they hadn't even asked her mom to come in for a meeting. By the time that Krista's mom actually did get home, Krista was feeling pretty good about things. She didn't even mind her mom's "What are you so smiley about?" Krista just shrugged and went to her room. Her mother didn't follow.

~ * ~

Harper couldn't hear exactly what her mother was saying to the principal, but she caught the tone and that pretty much filled in the rest. Harper just sat and looked at the wall, not wanting to make eye contact with either secretary while her mom may have been threatening to sue the school. There was a homecoming poster with Superman on it. So much for heroes, Harper thought. She supposed that she should probably listen to somebody's thoughts, but she'd hit a point of total exhaustion. The most intense pain had faded away and there wasn't an immediate threat, so her adrenaline had dropped down. After another couple of minutes, her mom came out of the principal's office. She knelt down in front of Harper and asked, "Are you okay, sweetie?"

Harper was glad that no other students were in the office to hear that. "I'll be okay, Mom."

Her mom looked at Harper for a few seconds, then she picked up Harper's backpack and stood. "Let's get going then. Your father should be home already."

Harper stood and tried to not look like she was steadying herself. Of course, her mom was watching her like a hawk. Harper gestured for her mom to go first. If she was leading the way, then she wouldn't be able to stare at her quite as easily. Her mother hesitated, then she went. Harper followed a little behind her, and her mom kept turning around to look every few seconds.

They didn't really talk much until they got to the car. Before starting the car, Harper's mom turned to her and said, "What happened? What really happened, Harper?"

Harper wasn't sure how to respond. She was sure that she'd have to give a second recounting to her dad, so she figured that it was best to be barebones here and expand a little at home. "I'm honestly not sure, Mom. This kid at lunch just went berserk."

Her mom nodded. "And you don't know why he decided to punch you?"

"Are you saying that I started it or something?"

Harper's mom touched Harper's forearm. She had to lean awkwardly to get over the little cup holder between the front seats. "No, honey, not at all. I just mean, I don't know. This boy never had said anything to you before? Had never done anything?"

"Not really. I mean, before he came after me, he was yelling at his friend, and then it's like he punched me just because I was there. Just because I was close enough to punch."

Her mom patted her arm. "I'm so sorry, Harper. I'm so sorry this happened."

Harper sighed. "Thanks, Mom. I appreciate that, but, really, I just want to go home."

"Of course," she started the car and backed out of her spot. "Is there anything that you want before we go home? Anything. Ice cream? A movie?"

Harper thought about it. It did seem like an opportunity that she shouldn't let slip away, but she also didn't feel like stopping anywhere. "No," she said. "I just want to go home."

They drove in silence for most of the way. Harper looked out the window, watching the town that was starting to look less familiar to her. Where did this rage come from? She was startled when her mother spoke.

"Harper," she said, "If you need a day or two off from school, we would totally understand."

Harper rubbed her eyes. After getting punched in the face, she could use a day off, but the thought of leaving James and Krista (assuming that Krista hadn't been suspended) was too much. Even beyond the concerns about the school's negative presence, Harper just wanted to know that her friends were okay. "I appreciate the offer," Harper said, "but school will be safer tomorrow than ever before. Everyone will be watching during lunch because the principal will have told everyone that the school can't afford to be sued. Tomorrow every cough or sneeze or blink will lead to a talk with the principal. A day at school a few months from now might be dangerous, but tomorrow will be the safest day in the entire history of the school."

Harper's mother turned to look at her for a few seconds, something she almost never did while driving. Then she said, "That's a very mature position to take, Harper."

Harper wasn't totally sure what to say to that. She was kind of proud and kind of not about hearing her mom tell her how mature she was. "Thanks," Harper said. "I'm trying," she said.

Harper's mom kept her eyes on the road then, and Harper got one of those rare moments where she could see her mom's point of view. There must have been a mix of terror and helplessness and, on a deep level of totally irrational thought, pride. A pride that might have been strong because it was absurd and dumb.

"We're here to protect you, Harper," her mom said. "Your dad and I want to protect you."

Harper found herself getting choked up. She had allowed herself to be upset at school. She figured that getting punched in the face earned her the right to panic and lose it, but she wasn't expecting to be upset at home, too. She thought it would mainly be answering enough questions to get her parents off her back and then sitting and listening to her parents talk about how the school had failed to protect her. This was different from what she'd expected. This was her recognizing that her parents were worried, and that they had good reason to worry. When they pulled into the driveway, Harper saw her dad standing by the front door. She felt herself starting to cry again.

~ * ~

James had made it through the rest of the day with limited difficulties. Now, at his locker, he saw something truly unsettling: Jenna.

She'd been outside of their central concerns for long enough that seeing her now was a genuine shock. She was standing and staring at him. James's first reaction was to look at the floor. His heart was racing, but he knew that he couldn't avoid eye contact for long. Jenna could be making some kind of move quickly. "Hello, Jenna," he said. "How are you?"

"Terrified," Jenna said. "I'd guess that everyone should be scared after today's lunch."

James held his backpack in front of him, and he pressed his back against his locker. He quickly looked at Jenna's face, then back down. "I don't know," he said. "The hot dogs weren't *that* bad."

Jenna gave an annoyed sigh. "Stick to being a freak, James. Leave the jokes to funny people."

James smiled. "You've laughed at me plenty of times before." He felt strange, almost giddy. He knew that it was stupid to rile the entity up like this but he couldn't help himself. He wondered if this was what Krista felt like most of the time.

"So you're not scared?" Jenna asked. James looked up. Jenna was looking at him without facing him directly. It actually seemed to match up with Jenna's typical attitude.

"You were right the first time," he said. "We should all be a little scared by what happened." James tried to calm himself while he spoke to her. He was alone, so his rational thoughts were all he had. He didn't expect that his power would have much sway over Jenna, even if she wasn't fully backed by the entity at the moment.

"Well," she said, "I guess you're just barely smart enough to listen. You should make sure to keep listening so that you don't end up getting hurt."

James wondered what that meant. Was this a recommendation to let himself fall under the influence of the chant that had controlled Brent? "I'm surprised to hear a popular girl like you espousing the values of conformity."

Something seemed to pass over her face. After a moment of quiet, she said, "What?"

Of all the possible replies, this was not the one he'd expected. It made him wonder if the entity was always limited by the vocabulary of its agent. "Why are you trying to help me out?" he asked.

Jenna shook her head. "I really don't care. You can hang out with the other weirdos tomorrow."

James looked at her carefully. Her posture was slumped, like typical Jenna. "If I'm back to my usual friends tomorrow, then tomorrow's company will certainly be a step up from the present one."

Jenna rolled her eyes. "Whatever. I'm not even sure why I'm talking to you."

"For once," James said, "you and I are very much in agreement."

Jenna looked around. She seemed confused, but she walked off without engaging James any further. At first, James felt uneasy. It seemed like this must be some kind of trick. But, as he looked down at his fingers, he realized something. He'd been tapping out a rhythm while he and Jenna had been talking. This was the same relaxation technique that he'd used when Jenna's friend had left him alone. Had he been using the exact same rhythm? It would be impossible to remember, but maybe there was something to go on now. There was at least a working hypothesis for him to have a real direction. After the disaster that had happened at lunchtime, James found himself very grateful for anything to give him some comfort.

~ * ~

Harper's parents had been surprisingly calm after talking about the incident. While they'd given her more assurances than were necessary, they also gave her a good deal of space once dinner was over. Harper went to her room. Rather than doing her homework like usual, Harper checked her email on her phone. She hadn't expected to hear anything from Krista, but she was a little sad to realize that she wouldn't be able to know how she was doing until tomorrow. James had sent a message. He told Harper that he hoped she was okay, that he wasn't sure how Krista was, and that he hoped to see her tomorrow. At the end he said that he thought he'd have something to tell her the next time that he saw her and he said it should set her mind at ease. Harper tried not to get her hopes up too much over that claim. For now, just being safe would have to be enough.

Harper looked at her phone. She knew that she should reply to

James, but she couldn't figure out what to say. Aside from not really knowing what would be helpful for him to hear, she wasn't sure who else was reading these emails. It didn't seem like the thing in control of the school would need to intercept emails to know what was happening, but she couldn't be sure that their phones wouldn't be seen by anyone else.

Harper clicked "reply" and stared at the blank message for a few seconds. "James," she wrote, "I'm doing all right. Thanks for reaching out. I don't know what happened to Krista, but she seemed to be in control of herself when I saw her in the principal's office. I'll be at school tomorrow. I look forward to hearing your news." She looked at it for a few more seconds before she decided that it was as good as it was going to get. She hit "send" and put her phone down.

She felt like staying home from school, and she also felt like she was being a baby for feeling that way. She wanted to show up to school and scream at everyone, and she wanted to be as invisible as Krista for the day. Most of all, she wanted to sleep and she wanted to not close her eyes, to be able to see her surroundings to feel safe.

Harper decided that she would at least try to do a little homework. There wasn't much else to do with her time. She opened her history book and tried to focus. She read about the aftermath of the Civil War until her eyes crossed. She picked up her phone and checked her email again. James had replied. He said that he was glad to hear that she was okay and that he looked forward to seeing her tomorrow. He hoped Krista would be there as well. Harper chuckled, then sighed. She hoped the same thing, but probably even more than James.

Harper stood up and stretched. She went down and said good night to her parents. She went through her nightly ritual of brushing her teeth, washing her face, and so on. When she went back to her room, she changed, turned out the lights, and got into bed. Then Harper stared at her ceiling for a very long time, but she did eventually fall asleep.

~ * ~

Krista wasn't sure what to expect when she got to school. It seemed like kids would stare at her a little, then go back to ignoring her, but she also didn't feel like she could be confident of much of anything lately. She thought about going into school invisible and turning visible in a bathroom, but there were too many different ways that it could go wrong, s o she just went in trying to avoid eye contact with anyone.

It worked through the parking lot and even through the front doors. Krista was sure that people were whispering or laughing or something, but no one stopped her or got in her face. Of course, as soon as she let her guard down, somebody did talk to her. It was that guy that had smiled at her the other day. When he saw her, he nodded to her and said, "Hey."

Krista nodded back, but she kept walking. The boy started to follow her. "Hey," he said again, "I thought what you did yesterday was cool. It was really badass."

Krista laughed out loud before she could stop herself. "Badass," she said.

Now the boy laughed. "No, really. It's cool that you protected your friend like that."

Krista smiled but kept walking. "Not to disappoint you, but don't expect a repeat performance."

The boy shrugged. "Once is probably enough. Besides, there might be other reasons to like you."

Krista rolled her eyes, "Yeah, I'm a real barrel of monkeys, all right."

"Well, Monkey Girl," he said, "stay safe in the lunch hall."

"I'd better stay away from the green beans, then." Almost immediately, Krista thought that she probably should have gone with "the egg patties," but she couldn't retell the joke.

The boy let her walk off. She resisted the urge to turn around and look back. By the time she got to her locker, she'd been able to shake off the paranoia of the morning. She didn't even worry about finding James and Harper. As she put her things in her locker, she let herself s mile. When she closed her locker door, her smile faded. Jenna had gotten inches from her without Krista noticing. Krista gasped.

"Hey loser," Jenna said. "Attack anybody yet this morning?"

Krista moved a little bit away. "Not yet," she said, "but it's still early, Jenna."

Jenna crossed her arms and tilted her head. "Is that a threat, weirdo?"

"I wouldn't have thought that a loser like me could be a threat to a cool kid like you, Jenna."

Jenna shrugged. "If whatever's wrong with your face is contagious, that could be dangerous."

Krista looked Jenna over. The insults she was giving were pretty standard Jenna insults. Maybe she wasn't being run by the school's demon today. "What do you want with me, Jenna?"

Jenna looked at her nails. "Just stay away from me, and stay away from my friends, okay?"

Krista knew that it couldn't be that simple. Was it just the thing running the school trying to intimidate her? "That's fine," Krista said, "I'm supposed to play it low-key today anyway."

Jenna walked away. This time, Krista let herself watch. She was back to feeling creeped out by the whole school. She tried to tell herself that this was a good thing, that this would make sure that she was focusing on finding James and Harper so that they could get to work. She walked to her first class looking at everyone she passed. Any of them could be a threat. Even worse, all of them could be the same threat. And on top of the threat of violence (maybe the thing running the school attacked Harper to see how she and James would react), she had to make up the work she missed after being sent home from school, and she had to keep an eye on communications from the school in case they tried contacting her mom again. By the time she got to first hour, Krista already felt exhausted.

~ * ~

The first part of the lunch period was pretty much quiet at their table. Nobody wanted to go first. Eventually, James asked Harper, "Does it still hurt today?"

Harper pulled the crust off her sandwich. "Not really. It feels like I have a terrible cold, I guess."

"Did you parents freak out?" Krista asked.

Harper chuckled. "All things considered, my parents were very cool about it. What about your mom?"

Krista shrugged and didn't say anything. She didn't want to be a jerk, but she also knew that if she admitted to not saying anything, there would be a debate about that instead of about what they needed to do next. "I don't see the guy who punched you here today."

Harper tossed her bread's crust on the baggie it came from. "I wouldn't worry about him too much. Whatever is causing all of this is smart. It'll use someone else the next time it attacks."

"Which of us do you think will be the next target?" James asked.

"It could be all of us," Krista said. "It could come for the three of us at once."

Harper looked around the lunch hall. There was the smattering of half-assed posters, and all of the kids in the hall. "There," she said. She was looking at the boy whose thoughts had spooked her so much. When she looked back, she saw James and Krista watching her carefully. "You feeling up to listening?" Krista asked. "Because, if you're not…"

"It's better to be cautious and healthy later than impetuous and in serious danger," James said.

Krista said, "Did you get that from a fortune cookie, James?"

Harper closed her eyes. Honestly, she was scared, but she was more scared of not knowing. "I'll do it," she said. Harper kept her eyes closed, and she tried to pinpoint the boy's thoughts. It took a minute to filter through the noise, but she eventually caught his voice. He had the same basic voice, but the content and the tone of his thoughts had changed completely. Today, he wasn't thinking about violence or aggression. Today, the boy was thinking about his fear and his despair. He was worried that people could tell what he was thinking. He was worried that he'd try to intimidate someone and just end up getting his ass kicked. Harper opened her eyes. "That's not what I expected to hear. It's like he's a dog that's been beaten for no reason."

Krista gave a short, sharp laugh. "If he got his ass beat, then I'd bet there was a reason."

"I disagree," James said. "Of anyone in the school, we should be able to sympathize with someone who feels isolated from their peers."

Krista rolled her eyes. "Yes, James, being hard of hearing should make me feel sorry for some able-bodied that wants to blow away all of our fellow classmates. You're so fair and wise."

After a brief silence, James said, "That was a pretty blatant misinterpretation of what I said."

"Both of you, shut up," Harper said. They both looked at her in surprise, and Harper sighed. "Look," she said, "we don't have to sympathize with everyone who's picked on. Some people do turn into jerks, yes. But what if he's genuinely struggling between being scared and sad and being driven to hatred by whatever awful thing is controlling everyone else? What if it's not really his fault?"

James was about to say something when an object hit his head. It was light, but it startled him anyway. When he jumped, there was laughter, but James didn't recognize its source. He looked at the ground. There was a wadded-up piece of paper. Harper said, "Just leave it."

James picked it up anyway. He unfolded the paper. In large letters, someone had written, "Cripple threesome." James felt his face turning red as he crumpled it back up. Krista held out her hand to see the paper, but James shook his head. "They're scared," he said. "It's trying to distract us."

"I think it's working," Krista said. "I can't deliver my usual level of wit in my comebacks."

Harper tore her sandwich in half. "James is right, we need to focus on a clear course of action before it starts to dominate us." She bit off a piece of the half in her right hand.

"We could try to befriend that scared boy," James said. "Maybe we could learn something."

"Waste of time," Krista said. "I say that we find another way to challenge it."

"Since you mention challenging," James said, "I may have found a way to free people from its influence, though I suspect that the freedom is only temporary."

"Holy crap, James," Krista said, "you have this and you didn't lead off with it?"

"I didn't want to overstate the potential. It's still largely untested and undefined."

"That's still better than most of what we have up to this point,"

Harper said.

"Okay," James said. "Twice now, I've been able to seemingly disrupt the control of the entity over students interacting with me. The common element in both cases was that I was tapping while they were trying to approach me. I believe that the tapping counteracts the chant that controls them."

"You were tapping?" Krista said. "What does that mean? Like you were dancing or something?"

"Tapping on a table or my legs can help to calm me," James said. "It's one of a number of techniques that I use in moments of elevated anxiety."

Before Krista could respond, Harper said, "Is there a specific beat that you use?"

"That's part of the issue, "James said. "The beat is almost involuntary. I'm not sure that I can intentionally reproduce it, and I'm quite sure that I wouldn't be able to teach it to others."

They were quiet again, then Harper said, "There's still some potential. Maybe if we recorded it, then the tapping could give all of us protection."

"How would we generate a sense of anxiety in me while maintaining a controlled environment?"

Krista smiled. "I think my talents are needed here." A second wad of paper came at the table. This one missed James's head and landed in the middle of the table. This time, Krista grabbed it. She opened it up to find a picture of what the first wad had described. She crumpled the wad back up. "You're right, James. This stupid thing is scared of us. And you know what? It should be."

~ * ~

At the end of the day, Harper felt exhausted. Beyond her not having slept well the previous night, she felt keyed up in both good and bad ways. All day, she'd resisted the urge to constantly be listening to other people's thoughts. While it would have helped her to know who was a threat, she was sure that it also would have made her paranoid. It made all of the hero decorations up at school seem ironic, like even the usual protectors were against her. They probably were.

Harper would have been listening for hints of the thing so hard that she would have become oblivious to her immediate surroundings. Even without listening in to thoughts, there was enough to be worried about. All day, there was nervous laughing and whispering. Not that she should be surprised. Yesterday had been a big (if terrible) event. Of course, people were talking.

But there was at least some reason to be hopeful. Tomorrow after school, the three of them would meet to record James's tappings. It felt like instead of just "observing," they were finally taking some kind of action. They could start fighting back soon. Now the trick would be to make sure that her parents wouldn't freak out if she wanted to not come home right after school. As low-key as they'd played things yesterday, Harper knew that, deep down, they were probably still in a panic. Harper reminded herself that any fears her parents had were actually rational. That meant that Harper would have to make it sound like her friends were a source of comfort without making her parents feel inadequate.

And so, as she climbed into her mother's car, Harper tried to appear upbeat and confident, the kind of girl who was grateful for a strong support network at home.

"How was your day?" her mom asked. She was looking at Harper in the rearview mirror.

Harper smiled and looked at the mirror. "Boring. Not a single noteworthy thing happened today."

Her mom chuckled. "Well, I'm sure that that was a welcome change of pace."

Harper resisted the urge to look out the window. If her mom didn't reference yesterday, then she didn't have to either. Not directly, anyway. "It was," Harper said. "For once, a boring day was nice."

They drove in silence for a while. Harper was thinking about whether it would be easier to talk to her mother individually about hanging out or if she should wait for her father to be in the room as well. Harper's mother interrupted her thoughts. "Do you have much homework tonight?

"Not much, and my teachers said that I don't have to have it done tomorrow." She paused. Her mother didn't look away from the road. "Still, I think I'm just going to get it done tonight. Why wait?"

"No time like the present," her mom said. Harper tried not to laugh. She supposed that she had her own dumb phrases she hung onto in bad times. With her next question, Harper's mother's voice got higher. The pitch reminded Harper of when she was young and her mother would try to tell her father that there was a spider in the room, but she would do it calmly, even cheerfully, so that Harper wouldn't freak out. "So," her mother said, "how did the kids at school treat you today?"

Harper understood what her mother was asking. "Pretty much like normal," she said. Harper was quiet a moment. When she did talk again, she tried to keep her voice steady, but she knew that it must have sounded just as awkward as her mother's. "I think that Krista felt bad for me. She wanted to know if I felt like doing something after school tomorrow."

"Oh," her mother said. "That was nice." A pause, then, "Is that something you want to do?"

Harper kept staring out the window, she didn't have to use her powers to know that her mother was looking at her. Harper tried to look like she was actually thinking it through. "I think so," she said. "Krista and I have been talking a lot lately, and it'd be nice to hang out outside of school."

"It does sound nice," her mother said. Harper had the awful feeling that handling these non-conversations was going to be a major part of adulthood. But that was a worry for a different day. For now, Harper was able to be part of the recording session without major drama. That felt like a win.

~ * ~

The school day had been relatively quiet. All three of them had endured minor harassment and aggravation, but that also gave them the feeling that they were onto something, that they were becoming a legitimate threat. It helped them all to keep things under control.

They knew that they couldn't meet anywhere in the school, and they didn't want to meet at any of their houses. Adding to that, most outside places would be too loud, so they settled on going to the public library and finding one of the little reading cubbies where people would sometimes work. It would be quiet enough to get a recording, and there was a good chance that no one would bother them. They split up after school and met at the library so nobody would see them.

When they got there, they decided that Krista would agitate James, James would tap on the table, and Harper would record it on her phone. It seemed simple enough. Part of the problem, though, was that the library was a quiet place and Krista could struggle with regulating her volume, After her first two attempts at insulting James only resulted in him saying, "What?" she said, "Take the cotton out of your ears and the stick out of your ass," a little too loudly. While the librarian shelving books didn't come over, she gave a harsh enough glare that they were all quiet again. Krista tried leaning in and whispering to James. "All those times that Jenna made fun of you, I actually thought she was really funny. I was laughing at you behind your back, James."

Harper couldn't hear what Krista said, but when Krista leaned back, Harper held her phone over towards James. But James just shook his head. "The problem here," he said, "is that I know how much you hate Jenna. Even if you thought that something that she said was funny, you wouldn't have laughed out of general principle." After a pause, he added, "And you probably don't hate me."

Krista looked at Harper and frowned. Harper said, "Well, he's not wrong, is he?"

Krista thought for a moment. She chewed her lip for a second, then she leaned in again. "Listen," she said, "I'm not going to insult you, but I'm going to be honest. If you don't start tapping, then we're screwed, so let the threat of Harper getting hit again, of either of us falling prey, or anything else be the thing that scares you into a tapping panic. Let it, or we'll all be dead."

Still, James didn't move. When he did respond, it was just to say, "I'm sorry."

At first, Krista looked angry. Harper was worried that she was going to slap James. Then, a flicker of a smile passed over her face. Krista moved even closer to James. She put her arm around him. With her other hand, she stroked James's hair. Harper was so dumbfounded that it took Krista kicking her under the table to understand what was happening. James was tapping the table very quickly. Harper held her phone up to James's hands, and she hit "record". After a full ten seconds, she paused. She was replaying the recording to make sure that she'd gotten it (she had) when the librarian came over to the table. She leaned in and said, "I'm not sure what kind of project you're working on, but I don't think the library is the place for it."

Krista patted James on the shoulder. "Our friend here is having a rough time at school."

Harper said, "I think we're ready to get going anyway." Harper looked at James and Krista and nodded, sliding her phone into her backpack and standing.

"We appreciate your patience," James said. He also stood and gathered his things quickly. Krista smiled and took her time. The librarian watched them the whole way out. Once the three of them got outside, Harper and Krista burst out laughing. This continued for a full block. When they had settled down, Harper said, "I got it. You can definitely hear the tapping. Now we just need to figure out what to do with it."

"First," said James, "we make sure that we all have access to it for defense purposes."

"So we all have our own recording to use to ward off threats?" Harper said.

"Yes," James said, "but we'll need to be careful. If the entity recognizes that we have a defense against it, then it will find new and even harsher ways to target us."

"Plus we'll look like weirdos chasing people with our phones," Krista said. "And I don't even have a phone."

James went on. "We might also try to study the recording. See if there's something to the rhythm or cadence that can help us try to find other defenses or weapons."

"You're just trying to get us to listen to your new hit song, aren't you, James?" Krista said.

"Fine," James said. "I'll listen to the recording myself. Probably, I'm more suited to pick up on the subtle patterns and repetitions than you are anyway."

Krista smiled. "James," she said, "was that a burn you just gave me?"

James shrugged. "I was mainly giving an accurate summary of our most pertinent skill sets."

"Sounds like a burn to me," Harper said. She smiled at Krista, who rolled her eyes. "So," she said, "While you're applying your skills to the recording, what do you think we should be doing, James?"

"We still need to reach the young man who felt so alienated. I also think it's worth talking to Jenna."

Krista said, "Talking to Jenna has never been worthwhile, but right now she's exceptionally worthless."

James started to tug at his ear a little. "While I agree that, as a person, Jenna leaves a good deal to be desired, I've begun to think that, as this entity branches out into different people, instead of stretching its power thinner, it actually grows. If this is true, then every time that it inhabits somebody…"

"We have less of a chance of stopping it," Harper said. They'd reached a corner where they'd have to decide whether they'd part ways or find somewhere else to go. Rather than acknowledge this, they just stopped walking.

"Okay," Krista said, "so if one of us really has to do it, then which of us is going on Jenna duty."

"I can try," Harper said. "I probably hate her a little less than you do, so it'll be a little less of a burden. But it wouldn't have to be just one of us, either."

Krista groaned. "But what if I just end up alienating her?"

"With your charming personality, that's simply not possible," James said.

Harper laughed. "Now that, my friend, is a sick burn." James gave an exaggerated bow and Krista just shook her head. "Okay," Harper said, "this is good enough for now. I'll get you both copies of the recording tomorrow, and we can start working on bringing people away from control." The other two agreed, and, after a little more chatting, they decided to part ways and talk again at lunch.

~ * ~

When Krista got home, her mother was in her room, watching TV. Krista could tell from the flickering light on the wall. She thought about just going to her room to do homework, but she decided that she should probably check in. It would let her mom know that she hadn't come home late, and she could get a sense of whether or not her mom had found out about her upcoming detention. So Krista went into her mom's room. After standing quietly for a minute, she knocked on the door frame. When her mom looked, Krista said, "Hey!"

Her mom said, "Hey," and went back to watching TV. She didn't really seem mad, just disinterested in her usual way, so Krista felt safe. She turned and started to go, but her mom said something. Krista couldn't quite tell what. She went back in so that she could watch her mom's mouth. "What?" she asked.

"I said why'd you get home a little late?" Her mom kept looking at the TV. It was some old game show.

Krista said. "I was talking with some friends is all."

Now, Krista's mom looked straight at her. "Friends, huh? Any of them a cute boy?"

Krista stopped for a moment, not entirely sure that what she heard was really what she thought she'd heard. "Oh my God, Mom," Krista said. "It was just a couple of friends and I talking, that's all."

Her mom shrugged. "I wasn't always the old lady you see sitting here watching TV."

Krista laughed. She tried to remember the last time her mom had really made her laugh. "Well," she said, "I'd rather watch TV alone than date most of the guys in my school."

"Suit yourself," her mom said, "but you should have a little fun while you're young."

"Okey dokie," Krista said. She wondered if her mom was dying or something. Krista left the room before they could talk more. She grabbed a few of the generic Oreos that her mom had bought and went into her room. Maybe it was just her mom's dumb question, but Krista started thinking about that boy again. The one that had called her a badass. Was he really interested? Was he teaming up with Jenna to pull a prank on Krista? Or did he just figure that she'd probably be lonely and desperate enough to screw any guy who seemed interested?

Krista sighed and twisted open the first cookie. She ate the half without any frosting. Maybe she could convince James or Harper that hanging out with him was giving the school good vibes. Maybe neither of them would really notice anyway. Krista unscrewed a second cookie and, again, she ate the no frosting half.

Krista pressed the two leftover frosted halves together. She told herself that she was only thinking about all this because her stupid mom made a stupid joke anyway. She told herself to put it out of her mind so that she could focus on whatever was going on in the school. Then she took a bite of the two halves that she'd pushed together. It was sugary and boosted her mood a little. She wouldn't go so far as to say that she was in a good mood, but she trusted that she'd survive, even if it was only to keep living a life of budget cookies and algebra homework; she and her friends would get through it.

~ * ~

Harper was flipping through her freshman yearbook. She was kicking herself for not looking at it earlier to find the boy who was so distraught. It's possible that he was new to the school this year, but she doubted it. After finding James's and Krista's powers by using her own, Harper had looked for others with powers, and, at the beginning of this year, she also tried to find the new students to check them out as well. She didn't remember seeing him as she searched through the handful of newbies. Of course, she wouldn't have known to be looking for him, but she suspected that he was probably shy. Or maybe alienated was a better way to put it.

She made it all the way to the R's before seeing his face. Steven Richards. He seemed forgettable. Harper couldn't really think of anything he'd done to set himself apart. At least now they had a name, though she realized that that didn't help her make an actual connection. Maybe if she used his name when approaching him, he would feel more at ease. Or maybe he'd just feel creeped out. Harper wondered if she could use her power to find out his daily schedule. Usually, she could hear thoughts, but she wasn't able to search those thoughts, to move forward or backward through them to find a piece of information. Instead, she was stuck with whatever was going through the minds of whoever she was listening to.

There was a knock and Harper jumped. "Woah," her dad said. "Sorry for startling you."

Harper laughed. "No big deal. I was just thinking, is all." She thought about closing the yearbook, but she thought that any movement would make her dad more likely to see what she was looking at. If he started asking her, she wasn't sure what she'd say. "Dinner almost ready?" Harper asked.

"That's what I came up to tell you," her dad said. In moments like these, Harper always was waiting for the other person to make a joke about her reading their minds. Luckily, that had only happened a couple of times. Usually people were more focused on what they were going to say or not say about her disability, though that led to a whole set of awkward jokes.

"Great," Harper said, "I'll be down in just a little bit."

"Okay," her dad said. He hovered there in her doorway. Harper quickly listened to his thought. It was pretty much what she had guessed. "Dad," she said, "I'm fine. I mean, it was a little weird today, but you don't need to worry about me."

Her dad smiled. "Honey," he said, "I'm your dad. It's my job to worry."

Harper smiled, "Well, you deserve a raise then." She felt the smoothness of the yearbook papers under her fingertips. She thought about all those faces that could have been hiding fear or hate or who knew what. She also appreciated her dad checking in, but she wished that he'd leave her room.

"Maybe I'll ask for one during my annual performance review," he said. Harper thought about making a joke about her mom being the boss, but she decided that the less they talked the more satisfied they'd be. Plus, it would have been pretty cliché. She smiled, but she also broke eye contact. After a second or two, her dad seemed to take the hint. "Okay, about ten minutes?"

Harper said, "Okay," then watched her father go. She flipped through a few more pages of the yearbook. There was Jenna smiling. There she was laughing. There she was acting shy. Harper grudgingly admitted to herself that Jenna probably felt a lot of pressure to perform. Maybe it was that desire for approval and need to be normal while also being exceptional that made her so vulnerable to whatever was running the school. Maybe James was much more insulated because he didn't have the same drives as most other teenagers. With Krista, it was tougher to say. She always seemed like she didn't care, but Jenna could seem that way on the surface. For Harper, she just tried not to worry about it. She never had a time when she was normal. She wasn't like Tommy, who would have to learn to be disabled when he came back to school. Her normal was cerebral palsy.

Harper closed the yearbook. She did some hand stretches, then she got up to head down to dinner. She could smell what it was from the stairs. Spaghetti. It could be worse. As Harper put a hand to the wall and headed down, she thought that could be the motto for the three of them: "It could be worse."

~ * ~

James was thinking about the rhythm. He was confident that he'd be able to translate it into a weapon. He could probably use any kind of basic programmable keyboard to produce a louder and more consistent version of it. It would even be possible to get it played over the loudspeaker with the efforts of Harper, Krista, and himself. The question was: what would they do once they had the entity under control? The fact that it seemed to change and respond to circumstances led him to believe that any mastery of it that they achieved would be temporary. So, they needed to find the real source of the entity's power so that they could move on it quickly while they had it powerless. Until then, they should use the recording they'd made only for defensive purposes and, even then, only in emergencies. Every time that they used it, they risked discovery.

James went back to his math problems, but he tapped his pencil as he read the directions. Maybe if he could get the rhythm to run through his head, he could be a walking shield against control. If it wasn't in moments of conflict, but at planned moments meant to test his theory, then maybe it would be too chaotic to be understood. Or maybe he could use the disruptions he caused as a hint of where the entity was strongest. Maybe he could build a map that would lead him right to where they should focus their attack.

Of course, these were hopes and guesses. He didn't even have the basic evidence to refer to any of these ideas as a hypothesis. But the recording at least gave them enough cover to start gathering information in a more calm and strategic fashion. They could start searching thoughtfully, knowing that they had a barrier of safety that they could stay behind. James pushed his math aside and took out a clean sheet of paper. He once again wrote "know" and "need to find". Under "to find" he wrote "source of power". After a pause, he wrote a third column. This one said, "Method of finding". He drew a line from "source of power" and extended it to the third column. He wrote "Map of disruptions". He stared at the paper, then in the second column, he wrote, "why now?" It was a very obvious question, but he realized that they hadn't really sought the answer for it yet.

James tried to think of what had happened recently that was different from previous years. There was the accident with Tommy, of course, but Jenna's behavior had preceded that. There was homecoming, but that happened every year. James swallowed and realized that the closeness of himself, Harper, and Krista was a novelty to the school.

Using this as a starting point, it was possible to hypothesize that the presence of the three of them had drawn the attention of the entity. While the idea couldn't be entirely dismissed, James was skeptical. The entity had seemed to come after them first, targeting Krista and making itself known when it could have avoided their attention. Unless, as they'd discussed, the point was to trick Harper into listening into a mind so that she herself would fall "under the entity's control." But if that was the entity's goal, then why not try to control Harper directly instead of trying to control her through somebody else? After pondering that, James wrote two more items under the "need to find" heading. The first was, "What does it know about us?" and the second was "*How* does it know about us?" Then, "Why do we have our powers?"

Up to this point (even before the entity's influence became clear) the three of them had never really discussed this topic. Last year, their freshman year, they were all just so shocked and then glad to meet other special needs students with powers that they hadn't spent much time or energy discussing the mechanics behind them. He wondered if this was more an effect of them simply accepting things, or if there were still some basic barriers among them. While he had a general sense of Krista's background from the way that she talked about her mother, there were still significant gaps in his knowledge of her and which he would not feel comfortable asking about. With Harper, there was no intimidation or awkwardness; he simply had never thought to ask. In all fairness, neither of them had ever asked much about his home or personal life either, and James felt that, of the three of them, he had the most logical excuse for not observing social niceties. James shook his head. None of that was important at the moment.

The problem, of course, was that any real testing of the nature of these powers would require sophisticated tools, and they couldn't trust anyone who would have access to those tools to not take too much interest in them. Perhaps a byproduct of their fight against the entity would be a deeper understanding of what they had and what they were. James tapped his pencil and wrote "has this ever happened before?" in the second column. He went back to his math problems. All he had to do for the next few in a row was to find the derivative of continuous, non-trigonometric functions. If only everything in life could be this easy.

~ * ~

Krista had woken up feeling strange. Not really sick, but a little tired and mainly like there was something that she was supposed to remember, but couldn't. Like maybe there was an assignment that was due today, but that she hadn't finished. She did a quick mental run through of her classes and decided that, whatever she'd forgotten, it wasn't an assignment. Krista decided that whatever she'd forgotten would find her later in the day. She got dressed and went to the kitchen. Her mom was either asleep or gone already, Krista couldn't tell. She rummaged through the kitchen and eventually settled on some crackers and peanut butter for breakfast. She looked around the living room, but she still wasn't able to figure out what she might be either missing or forgetting.

After eating, Krista gathered her things, took one more look around, and headed to school. She got there a little early, so she wandered the halls, keeping an eye out for the depressed kid. She told herself that she'd talk to Jenna, too, if she ran into her. But she knew that she probably wouldn't as long as she stayed away from the hallway of popular jerks, and the depressed kid would most likely not be there if he didn't want to feel any worse about himself.

Krista passed the usual groups of dorks and/or jocks. She was just about to go to her locker when she saw the kid. He was sitting in front of what must have been his locker and writing on his shoe. Even if she hadn't been looking for the kid, Krista probably would have stopped to look. He was putting some kind of pattern around that white part on the bottom border of his shoe. Krista was smiling when the kid looked up. "What?" he said.

Krista shrugged. "Just admiring the work of a promising young artist."

The kid looked back down at his shoe and kept coloring his shoe. He said something quietly, and Krista had to say, "What?" The kid looked up again. He looked pissed off this time. Krista wondered if he was fantasizing about killing her. She turned her head, pulled her hair back, and pointed at her ear. The kid squinted. He looked at Krista and she let go of her hair. She watched the kid's mouth. He said, "I said 'Take a picture, it'll last longer.'"

Krista nodded. "It's a good thing you're a visual artist and not a stand-up comic."

The kids said, "Who'd want to try that with you around as competition?" and then he went back to his design. Krista went to the locker next to his and leaned against it. "Any significance to your design?" she asked.

The boy turned towards Krista. When he saw that she was looking at his face, he said, "Yeah. It's the universal symbol for 'go away'."

Krista nodded. "That's too bad," she said, "because I enjoy

annoying people, so now I pretty much have to sit here and keep talking to you." The boy looked at her again. Krista said, "Gotta do what you love."

"Shouldn't a deaf girl like silence?" the boy said. Krista watched his face. He didn't appear to feel guilty.

"You think a person in prison wouldn't love to see the outdoors?" After a pause, she added, "Even if it was full of bears and wolves and dumbass chimps who like to color on their shoes?"

The boy almost smiled, then he stopped. "You don't get out into the woods much, do you?" he asked.

"No," Krista said, "I waste too much of my time indoors, talking to chimps who draw on their shoes." She tilted her head and shrugged. She looked back at the boy's face.

"What?" he said. "You're leaving now?"

Krista shrugged. "I've successfully annoyed you. I believe that my work here is done."

The boy shook his head. "You're a real weirdo," he said. "You know that?"

Krista laughed. "I can't think of anyone who would know what normal is like you do."

The boy looked like he was going to say something, but then he just shook his head and went back to coloring. Krista headed to her locker. Even though the boy was kind of a jerk, she had a good feeling about him. Saving Jenna would be a long and annoying road to go down, but watching out for this weirdo could at least be entertaining.

~ * ~

Krista had gone into lunch prepared to do a little showing off. "So," she said, "I had a little conversation with that depressed kid. You know, the one that you two told me to keep an eye on."

"Oh," Harper said, "You're talking about Steven Richards?"

Krista felt her jaw almost drop. She narrowed her eyes a little. "How did you find out what his name is?"

"I have my ways," Harper said. After seeing Krista stink-eye her, Harper said, "I looked through the yearbook last night."

James put a hand over his eyes. "I can't believe that I didn't think of that."

"In all fairness," Harper said, "We all had a lot to worry about the past few weeks. I'm not sure that any of us were able to focus like we normally would."

"You're trying to be kind," James said, "but we need to hold each other to a high standard. If we're going to save each other and the whole school, then we can't overlook the obvious. And we can't tell each other that it's okay."

"Yes, Mom," Krista said.

James frowned, and Harper said, "No, I get it. We need to be smart."

"Okay," Harper said, "So tell us what kind of intelligence you've gathered on Steven."

Krista looked at James, then Harper. "He likes to draw designs on the white parts of his shoes," she said.

James said, "I am less than impressed," and he took a bite of his sandwich.

If Harper hadn't promised to only read their minds when it was absolutely necessary, then she would have listened to Krista's thoughts to see what words were behind her facial expression. "On the upside, maybe we can now say that we know both his name and where his locker is. That's not a total lack of progress."

"What kind of major breakthroughs have there been on the tapping front?" Krista asked James.

He explained his idea of mapping out the school. "Since we're making a point of stating the obvious," Krista said, "do we want to actually get a map of the school to start from instead of drawing one from scratch?"

"Yes," James said. "That's exactly what we need to start with. Good thinking, Krista."

Harper watched Krista. She looked down at the table and let herself smile slightly. "So," Harper said, "We have a sense of what needs to be done. Krista and I will keep on with Steven, though we should do it carefully, not too obvious for either Steven or the thing, and James will focus on making the map."

"There's one other point that we might want to discuss," James said.

"We should probably be keeping track of any aggression from the entity, even small things, so that we can both predict upcoming attacks and get a sense of what seems to threaten it most. So, have any of us seen anything unusual?"

Harper said, "I haven't had anything since the punch. I'm not sure if that's because the thing feels like it's scared me enough or if it just doesn't want to attract attention, but I've been safe."

James nodded. "I haven't had anything noteworthy happen. Krista?"

Krista narrowed her eyes a little and frowned. "I don't know," she said. "I can't point to anything specific, but I've felt weird all day. Not really sick or like a clear sense of doom or anything, but just…weird."

"When did you start noticing it?" Harper asked.

Krista thought about it. "Definitely it was there this morning, but even last night, my mom was acting weird. Like, weird for her, not just the usual 'I'm off in my room and grumbling to myself about whatever' kind of weird, but like something else. Or maybe I was just starting to feel it even yesterday."

"Let's not be too quick to ignore it," James said. "Did it happen in your home?"

"No," said Krista, "It happened while my mom and I were collecting flowers for a wedding bouquet. Yes, it happened at home."

James touched his left ear. "That would make it the first sign of control off school grounds."

"If it was actual control," Harper said. "Like Krista said, it could have been a number of things."

"Okay," James said, "I just think it's better to be watching carefully, than it is to be surprised."

"Was there anything else out of the ordinary these past few days?" Harper asked.

Krista's cheeks reddened a little. "Not really," she said. "Nothing to worry about or anything."

While Harper was still considering how much to pry into that, James said, "That sounds unconvincing."

Krista's face turned an even deeper shade of red. "Well sorry, detective. What evidence should I produce?"

James blinked and sat up straighter. "I was simply expressing concern."

"Right," Krista said. "You were concerned that I might have something that was my own business. And that's some kind of crime or something, right detective?"

"Relax" said Harper. She put a hand on Krista's forearm. "We're just trying to have each other's backs."

Krista rolled her eyes and stopped talking. "I'd never violate your privacy" James said. "If there's something you don't want to talk about…" He stopped and watched Krista. Since she was looking away, he wasn't sure if she'd caught what he'd said. When he looked over at Harper, she simply shook her head. He did have a general understanding of why he should stop, but it still seemed like a bad note to end lunch on.

But if he thought that was a bad note, then he only needed to look over at Jenna's table. When he did, he saw her smiling. When she saw him looking, she smiled and blew him a kiss. James was so shaken that he nearly fell over. Krista put a hand on his shoulder. "James," she said, "is there anything that *you* need to tell us?"

~ * ~

On the walk from lunch to her locker Harper had been able to convince Krista that she should talk to her after school, maybe away from James at first, so that Harper could smooth things over later. Harper wasn't sure what she was expecting, but she was a little surprised when Krista said, "There's kind of a boy."

"You didn't have to get defensive about that," Harper said. "Were you worried that James would be jealous?"

Krista laughed a little. "There's not much to be jealous of. He's just talked to me a few times, but there's a vibe there. Not that it matters. We can't afford to be worrying about that right now."

"Well, it's at least one more reason to keep fighting this thing, right?" Harper said.

"I've been thinking about that," Krista said. "We still don't really know what this thing's ultimate goal is."

Harper raised her eyebrows. "You think it's not bad? You think it's going to bake us cookies?"

"No," Krista said "but if it's part of the school, if it's in a lot of us, then is it actually going to destroy all of us or the school? Doesn't it need us to feed off of us?"

Harper frowned. "I guess that's true. But I still feel like we should be fighting it. Right?"

"Right," Krista said. She nodded towards someone. Harper looked in that direction. There he was, Steven, and he was coloring on his fingernails while other kids went into their lockers right next to his.

"Hey," Krista said, "You're working your way up. Next you'll be painting your face."

Steven looked around. It took him a minute to realize who'd said it. When he did, he looked back at his nails and shook his head. Harper laughed quietly. "You can do our nails next," she said.

"I won't do your nails," Steven said, "but I'd be happy to give you the finger."

Harper listened to his thoughts. He was mostly scared, though a little excited, too. Harper felt a little sorry for him, having to act invulnerable and aloof. Although he didn't think it directly, Harper could tell by his tone that this didn't come naturally to him as it did to Krista.

"Keep your finger," Krista said "You'll need your whole hand to keep yourself company."

Harper elbowed Krista gently. Krista didn't look at her, but she made her face a little more relaxed. Harper said, "We were just joking around. Don't let it get to you."

Steven stared at Harper for a moment. "Yeah," he said, "I wasn't planning on caring, to be honest."

Harper nodded. Steven was not being honest. Krista went towards the lockers. She stood next to a group of guys that were hovering around the lockers and talking. She stood very close and stared at them. Harper reached into her backpack's front pocket and put a hand on her phone. She thought she might need the recording. But after a few seconds of Krista's staring, one of the boy's said, "What's wrong with you?"

Krista let a smile spread over her face slowly, then she said, "I'm a danger to myself and others." The boys mumbled to each other, but they left. Krista turned to Steven. "You're right," she said, "not caring is easy."

Harper listened to his thoughts again. It was a mess of feelings. He was impressed with Krista for being able to pull it off so easily, he was annoyed that she had been able to do it so easily, and he was suspicious of why they were helping him in the first place. What he said out loud was, "My hero."

Krista opened her mouth, then she closed it and just shrugged. Harper breathed a sigh of relief. "Enjoy your locker access," Harper said. "No need to say thanks." she took Krista's arm and led her away before Krista could say anything. After they went on a little way, Harper said, "Well, that went well."

"I think he's growing on me a little bit," Krista said. "Even though he's kind of a dink."

Harper leaned in close to Krista. "How did you know that he wanted to get into his locker?"

Krista raised her eyebrows. "I borrowed your power and read his mind."

Harper laughed and shook her head. "Fine, don't tell me that. Tell me a little more about the guy who's been talking to you."

Krista looked around the hall before speaking. "Not a lot to tell. He told me that I'm a badass for punching out the guy that punched you. So that's either funny or kind of weird."

Harper smirked at her. "So you've been a badass and a hero. You're on a roll."

Krista shrugged. "All that snark and bitterness was bound to pay off eventually." They were quiet the rest of the way to the school's front doors. When they got there, Harper asked, "Want a ride home?"

"Nah," Krista said. "I mean, thanks, but sometimes the time walking alone is nice."

Harper nodded. "Well, enjoy," Krista didn't respond, so Harper didn't move. They stood there for a bit, with different kids either rushing past or stumbling by while looking at their phones.

Krista said, "Do you think James is right about this thing finding a way into my house?"

It's not what Harper was expecting. The truth was that she'd kind of forgotten about it, but she realized that Krista had to go home to it now. "I don't know," she said. "I don't know how it would get into your home if it hasn't gotten into anyone else's."

"Yeah," Krista said. "I guess I'm just the luckiest girl in school, or something."

"Do you want to come over tonight? I mean, you could come over any night."

Krista smiled. "I appreciate it, but I'll be all right. Besides, if it is in my house somehow, then I should try to observe it, right? We all need to be figuring this thing out."

"Yeah," Harper said, "but you need to be able to sleep and feel safe, too, right?"

Krista shook her head. "I'm a badass, remember?" With that she made her way out of the school.

~ * ~

To say that James's effort to map out the school that day was a good first step would be generous. Even James would admit that. The problem was that he'd not accounted for the difficulty of deciding who was under the entity's control. With Jenna and her friends, there was no problem, but, given James's particular limitations, determining who was behaving or emoting in an abnormal way was just too difficult, and playing the clip for the entirety of his walk through the hall seemed an unworkable solution that would lead to too much attention. He would need to try it again with Harper.

Rather than writing the walk off as a total failure, James decided that, on the last part of his circuit, he'd track the symbols of the school. There were the ubiquitous images of mascots and the smattering of superhero decorations that had been put up for homecoming, but today, when he stopped to look at the trophy case, James noticed something that he'd never seen before. While the most recent photos of teams and individuals did feature the current mascot, there were also older photos where the team jerseys said "Savages." In fact, James was surprised by how many of them there were.

He realized that he must have been staring at it for a while when he heard someone say, "Sorry, but they don't give out trophies for 'creepiest freak in the school.'"

James looked over to see the two football players from his English class. He couldn't tell, just looking at them, if they were working for the entity or on their own. "I wouldn't expect you to know this, but they do give out certificates of achievement for math club," James said.

"Guess we were wrong," the second football player said. "There are awards for biggest dork in school."

"I'm not a member of the club, personally," James said. He knew that he shouldn't have engaged the football players at all. Luckily, they simply walked past him, bumping into him as they went. It was after they'd gone that James realized that he should've played the clip to see how it impacted their behavior. This lack of quick reaction was another good reason to bring Harper along for the mapping process. Maybe Krista as well. While she sometimes had difficulties keeping her temper in check, she was able to react quickly. The larger question was whether the three of them were too likely to attract the entity's attention.

The good news was that he had all night (at least) to consider this. James sighed and headed to the back of the school, where his mother would be waiting for him. He made his way out without any other encounters. He saw the football players trickling out in their uniforms. The two who had ridiculed him didn't appear to be there, but it was hard to tell. James pictured himself playing the clip over the loudspeakers at a game. Would the whole football team be dumbfounded? What about the people in the stands?

James saw his mother's car. He wondered how long she'd been waiting. He looked around the parking lot, making sure there were no threats. When he made his way over and got in the car, his mother said to him, "You a little late getting out today, sweetie?"

James took this to mean that she was experiencing a minor level of annoyance. "Sorry," he said, "I got held up a little by a couple of slower students in the hall."

His mother turned around and watched him get in. "Is everything all right?"

"Sure," James said. "It was an inconvenience, but nothing that warrants actual concern." James felt that this statement was not a direct lie, even if it wasn't the entire truth. It was as honest as he could be.

His mother said, "Other than the slow down at the end, how was your day?"

"Good," James said. He knew that more specific material would help to set his mother's mind at ease, so he said, "We'll be switching over from differentiation to integration math soon."

His mother smiled. "Well, that'll be an exciting day."

"Well," James said, "It'll beat sitting through a pep rally for the football team, anyway."

James's mother laughed. "I'd just as soon skip both and curl up with a good book."

"Mrs. Benson always says that a book can be your best friend." Even as he said it, James felt like his mother would interpret it, would hear it in the suggestion that James was incapable of developing and maintaining close relationships with his peer group.

But if this was what his mother's reaction was, then she didn't show it. Instead, she simply said, "That's certainly a positive outlook to take." James and his mother were both quiet for the rest of the ride home.

~ * ~

Harper hadn't wanted to look at the text message when she first heard the ding. Of the several things that it could be, no positive possibility sprang to mind. It could be James alerting her to a potential danger, or it could be one of those stupid "school alerts" that let her know that the busses would be late tomorrow or that something in the school was malfunctioning and it would be her responsibility to plan ahead. But even if she didn't want to read the text, she owed it to the other two to not ignore something that could be important. When she checked, it was indeed from James. It read: "Your help in the mapping project would be appreciated." Looking at the wording, Harper thought she at least could trust that it sounded like James.

She picked up her phone and stared at it. Then she played a game of Panda Pop. She failed to save two of the baby pandas. She sighed and simply texted back, "When?"

She started to do her hand stretches. If her parents checked in, it wouldn't look like she was just waiting by the phone. She'd finished the first round of them and was doing some pincer work when a text came in. "Tomorrow would be optimal." Harper laughed a little. It sounded like a bumper sticker or a line on the bottom of the poster. Harper texted back "Have 2 check with parents." Then, "After school?"

This time, the response was almost immediate. "Or during" Harper was surprised. It must be something impressive if James thought they should be wandering the halls together during the school day. Or maybe he just figured that the rush of students would give them a little more cover than after school. She just texted back "K," then she set her phone aside and went back to her pincer work. It made her think of when she was a child. She'd do these exercises by picking up M&Ms with just her thumb and index finger, eating every tenth one. Now, she used little steel marbles that were bigger than the M&Ms but were also heavier. And the only reward was maintaining what dexterity she had.

Harper looked at her phone. No reply, which was fine. When the three of them had first started interacting, when she let them both know that she knew their thoughts and their powers, they never would have asked to borrow each other's powers. It was cool to see them at work, but that was as far as it went. Now, she wondered if either Krista or James felt that the requests for each other's powers were intrusive. She herself felt a little irked by James's presumption, but she also knew that he just saw it as being efficient, that wasting her time with chitchat would be annoying.

Harper dropped one of the marbles. It rolled off her desk and under her chair. She got up and moved the chair, but, when she did, she just bumped the marble again, and it went under the desk. She sighed and got down on all fours, reaching for it. She felt some dust, then what might have been an old potato chip (she decided to leave that, because she was not in the mood to deal with it today), and finally, the marble. She swept her hand towards her, bringing the marble out. At first, she was just going to pick it up with her left hand, but then she decided to try it with her right. She gripped the marble with her thumb and forefinger and picked it up. She put her left hand below it, in case the marble dropped again. It didn't. She was able to get the marble all the way to the little cup that she kept them in. It was all a matter of consistent focus and grasp that wasn't either too firm or too weak.

~ * ~

Krista had gone through her mother's things before. She knew that some stuff (pretty much the whole underwear drawer, for instance), was off limits, but there was also plenty of stuff that Krista could snoop through without getting caught. In the early going, just the fun of going through her mom's stuff had been enough to make it worth the risk, but that also meant that she hadn't always looked at things carefully and had gotten yelled at. Krista would be very careful putting everything back today. She developed a careful sense of how disorganized the right amount of messy would be. But in terms of catching everything that was in her mom's closet, she'd been kind of lazy, to be honest.

So now, she was staring at what she should have known was there for a long time. It could also easily be the thing that explained why her mom was affected at home and not just on school grounds. There, hanging in her mom's closet, was a varsity jacket. Along the back was the team name. Savages. Krista felt the sleeve. It was old and beaten up, but if you touched it in the right places, you could still find a smoothness to it. Krista tried to decide what to do with it. It would be great if she could just get rid of it, but the chances of her mom not noticing that seemed pretty small. She could try to somehow play the recording of James tapping either in the closet or somewhere in her mom's room, but how would she keep it going constantly? Maybe James or Harper would have a better idea. In the meantime, Krista had to live in the house knowing that her mother was being influenced by something that was basically her enemy. She tried to make herself smile by saying that that was basically every teenager's problem, but, this time, that didn't cut it.

Krista closed the closet as quietly as she could, then she went to the kitchen, moving quietly but steadily, she kept looking at the front door as she moved. She started going through the cupboards grabbing things (cheap cookies, a few pretzel rods, the jar of peanut butter) so that she could hide out in her room as much as possible. When she felt like she had enough, she went into her room and closed the door. At first, she just stared at the food. She knew that tomorrow she'd feel sick to her stomach, but there was still something comforting about having all the familiar junk food with her. Krista let her breathing slow down a little. She decided to get up and do a little homework. She'd have to get it done eventually, and maybe it would pass the time.

Krista started with math, which was probably a mistake. The first problem was about ratios and making a recipe. It was simple enough, but it also made her want to bust into the cookies right away, which would be a bad idea. She knew what her mom would say about all the junk food if she saw it, but it's not like either of them were about to make a gourmet meal.

Krista thought back to the jacket. Maybe she could cut the name off the back without her mother noticing. She might notice the jacket being entirely gone from the closet, but did she ever really look at it? Krista pictured her mother trying it on for old time's sake or something, and it creeped her out. Maybe Krista could claim that she wanted to borrow it for some costume project for school and just see if it really did make a difference for a day or two. But where would she keep it? Not in her own locker. With her luck some weirdo under the thing's control would break in and steal it. Though maybe that could be its own kind of blessing. Maybe the best idea was just to wait to hear what Harper and James said.

She'd actually started to make some progress on the math (she used those dumb tables of measurements that were printed on the pockets of her folder) when there was a knock on her door. She put her worksheet over her snacks and the jar of peanut butter behind her pillow, then she went to the door. She opened it, and her mom was there. Her mom's eyes seemed out of focus or something. She said, "Did you hear about some big fight at school?"

Krista took a second to steady herself. She kept looking at her mother's lips, hoping that it appeared like she was trying to figure out what her mom had said. "A fight?" Krista asked, "You mean today?"

Her mom shook her head, "No, more like a few days ago. It was at lunch I heard."

Krista wondered where her mother possibly could have heard about it. "Oh that," she said. "Yeah my friend got punched in the face by some braindead jerk for no reason. It was freaky."

"Someone punched your friend right in the face? And where were you?"

Krista started tapping on her leg with her left hand. She was sure it wasn't the same beat that James used but she thought she'd try something. "I was there," she said, "I tried to step in and help my friend. Tried to protect her as much as I could, but everything happened so fast."

"Is that right?" It was hard to say what her mom was thinking. "Anybody get in trouble?"

Krista could feel her cheeks heating up, but she made herself keep watching her mother's mouth. "I've got to go in for a detention. Next Monday."

"Really? And when were you going to tell me that?" The problem was that this was actually a reasonable question. That made it harder to be a smartass.

"I'm sorry," she said. "I should've just told you right away," Krista said. She watched her mom, trying to see if her reaction would say anything about whether it was really her mom asking the questions or if it was the thing that was running the school.

Her mom cocked her head to the side and narrowed her eyes. "You don't have a smartass comment to make?"

"I know," Krista said. "It probably seems like your daughter is under some kind of mind control." Not having a big reaction after saying that was very hard for Krista. She was used to mouthing off and keeping a straight face, but saying something that laid the cards on the table was different.

After a few seconds her mom looked her up and down and then just rolled her eyes. "Well, just don't start thinking that you can put one over on me. And what's with the tapping?"

Krista stopped the tapping. "Just a nervous habit or something."

Krista's mom turned halfway out of the door. "Maybe you wouldn't be nervous if you didn't keep secrets"

"I know," Krista said. Then, "Mom, I really am sorry. And I love you."

Krista's mom smiled and shook her head. "You weren't kidding about that mind control." She walked out of Krista's room. Krista watched her go, then she let out a long, slow breath.

~ * ~

The next day at lunch, Krista was telling the other two about the jacket and her mother. James said, "This is helpful. It tells us where we need to focus the recordings."

"Kind of," Harper said. "I mean, it does, but there are still a lot of questions that we can't answer."

"True," James said. "How do we keep the recordings going constantly? How do we ensure that it continually disrupts the entity's influence upon the school?"

"Sure, there's that," Harper said, "but there's also the question of why it's happening now?"

"And why it is that the tapping messes with this thing in the first place," Krista said.

James touched his ear. "Those are definitely good questions," he said. "But maybe we should keep our focus on stopping it for now, and we can figure out things later."

"I don't know," Harper said, "Shouldn't we understand what we're stopping to know how to stop it right?"

"My feeling," said James, "is that we should take care of the more immediate need first." He took a drink of his water.

"That seems surprising," Krista said. "Usually you want to do things like they are a homework assignment, but on this, you want to rush through things? What if you only get a C?"

Harper said, "Really though, there could be some serious consequences. Like what if we shut it down in the school then it gets worse in Krista's home or the home of anyone else with Savage crap in it?"

"I suppose that's a concern. And how would we track all of the memorabilia in town to ensure that any energy or control from the school doesn't show up there? If that's even how this works."

The three of them sat in silence. Krista was starting to feel panic coming on, not knowing what would happen with her mother. James was trying to organize his thoughts, to get a sense of where his motivations were coming from. Was it logic or fear? Harper was considering listening to the other two's thoughts. They all ate and avoided eye contact for a bit.

"Okay," Krista eventually said. "We've got to do something. James, are you ready to start working on your map stuff?"

"My map stuff," James said. "I tend to think of it more seriously than that."

"My bad," Krista said. "James, is there any way that you could allow your fabulous and world-saving project to be used for our sad little purposes?" Krista put her hands together, like a prayer.

"This is not the most effective way to bring me onto your side," James said.

Harper put one hand on Krista's arm and the other on James's. "Stop it," she said. "Let's think about how we can collaborate, not how we can get on each other's nerves."

James said, "Harper, how far can your powers extend? Could you reach to Krista's house?"

Harper shook her head. "I doubt it. I can operate within the school pretty easily, but even from here to the football field can be hard to know whose thoughts I'm hearing."

"What if you were over at my house and James was here, texting you?" Krista said.

"That could work," said James, "though we'd have to figure out where I'd try it and we'd also have to make sure that your mother was home at the time when the school was full."

"Sounds to me like James is asking us to play hooky, Harper," Krista said. She flashed a big smile.

Harper shook her head, "Sounds fun up until the point where my parents find out and kill me."

"Duh," Krista said, "that's why we all make sure that you don't get caught. Powers, and stuff."

"This is all pointless if we can't make sure that Krista's mom is in the house anyway," James said.

There was a bit of quiet again. The next person to speak was one of the lunchroom monitors, who had made her way over to the three's table. "So," she said, "no fistfights today?"

"Hey," said Krista, "we're the good guys. We never start fights."

"Maybe," said the monitor, "but it seems like you don't back down. Right?"

There was a little pause, then Krista said, "My mamma didn't raise no fool, if that's what you're asking."

James said, "We're always on the side of fairness is what she's saying."

The monitor looked at each of them, one at a time. "You know," she said, "I went to this school as a student. I've been here a long time and I know what this school is all about. I know who makes trouble, and I know how to watch people. So you three just keep that in mind. Don't make trouble, or who knows who might end up getting hurt."

"We understand," Harper said, "and thanks for your concern." The monitor stared at them a few more seconds before moving on. When she'd gone out of earshot Harper spoke quietly, but she faced Krista and she spoke slowly, making sure that she could read her lips. "That shows what we have to do now."

Krista and Harper spoke at almost the same time. Krista said, "Shut the school down now."

And Harper said, "Slow things down."

They looked at each other with a clear sense of surprise. James shook his head. "Incredible. We were moving in a clear direction, and then the entity comes along and, with just a few sentences, turns us against each other." Harper and Krista looked over at the monitor. She was talking to a group of boys at another table. It didn't look like she was thinking about what she'd just said to the three of them. Not even a little. "Okay then, genius," Krista said. "Bring us together. Tell us what we should be doing to fight this thing and still stay safe."

James looked down at the table. "I wish I could say that I know for sure. I really do. The fact that we were just warned could well imply that we're in a place of real power and control. But it could also just mean that we're being watched. If it's the first case, then we should press on. If it's the second, then we should be careful."

Krista rolled her eyes and looked away, which Harper knew was the end of the debate. She'd won, but her win came at the price of an angry Krista. James was right, the thing had divided them.

"Let's strike the middle ground between your reactions," James said. "Gather some intelligence and then move forward in a careful and logical way." Harper looked at Krista, if she had caught what James had said, then she would probably make a crack about the phrase "gather some intelligence." She didn't say anything.

"Okay, James," Harper said, "we'll map and Krista will pout. That suits our skill sets."

James nodded, but he didn't make eye contact. For all of the progress that they'd made, it didn't feel they were all that close to beating this thing.

~ * ~

After school, Krista had decided to be invisible for a while. Part of it was to just be left alone. She didn't want to have to talk to anyone, to make stupid conversation just to be polite, to have to focus and catch enough words to make sense of what someone was saying. The other reason was that she just liked being invisible every so often. She liked to know that it was still there. But it was getting colder outside and she wasn't sure how long she'd be able to stand it. Not that she had anywhere to go.

She'd wandered around a bit, strolling through the park. There weren't any kids there today, so she decided to climb into the branches of a tree. It was low enough that she could just sit there and watch everything and never got noticed or bumped into or anything. She'd put her backpack in a little fork off from the main trunk and a little above where she was. It really was calming to be up there. When she exhaled, she could watch her breath leave her body. She did that a couple of times and then she realized how stupid she was being. Anyone could walk by and see little puffs of her breath magically coming from the tree. It was time to get down.

Krista grabbed her backpack and gently plopped it on the ground.

Next, she dropped to the ground herself. It was a short drop, but she still had to crouch hard when she landed. She was about to turn visible again when a group of boys started crossing the park. Krista quickly moved her backpack behind the tree. She stepped mostly behind it, too, and she covered her mouth, making sure that her breath didn't give her away.

The boys were laughing, laughing at something stupid and boyish no doubt. As Krista watched them get closer, she recognized the boy. Her boy. She peeked a little further out from behind the tree. One of the other boys punched her boy in the arm. Then he laughed and punched the first boy back. They all laughed again. As they got closer, Krista wondered why any girl would date boys their age.

They'd walked most of the way through the park, still laughing and goofing off. Before they made it all the way out of the park, Krista's boy turned around. He looked almost exactly where Krista was standing. Krista pressed her hand tighter over her mouth. She shivered just a little. After a few seconds that seemed like an hour, one of the other boys pulled Krista's boy away. Krista stood there for several minutes before she picked up her backpack and turned visible. She walked home quickly, shivering the whole way. The rest of the night, she wasn't able to shake the feeling of being very, very cold.

~ * ~

Harper had always thought of herself as mentally strong, emotionally strong. If there were things that she couldn't do physically, she would find ways around it, even if it meant doing more than everyone else. It was part of who she was. Her parents had told her several times about how, as a small child, she would always find a way to get her right hand to help her open candy packages. And she had some memory of all the physical therapy she was stuck doing after her foot surgery when she was younger.

So it was all the more disappointing to herself that she was so easily shaken. In the hall after school, three boys running through the hall almost knocked her to the ground. They might well have not even known what they were doing. They ran into her and kept going. If she'd known that they were coming, she might have been able to brace herself, but, as it was, they ran into her and she almost totally crumpled. When she did, the sense of panic from being punched a couple of days ago came rushing back. She leaned hard against the wall and put a hand over her heart.

She found herself wishing that she had James's power so that she could trip the boys and watch them fall on their face. She wanted to be able to see them feel terror at being powerless. But she couldn't do that. She didn't have the power. And even worse, she had to watch the boys run off knowing that they were completely oblivious to what they'd done, and that they always would be.

Harper slowly pushed herself up and looked around. There were a few of the other students looking at her and then looking away. Harper could feel her face turning red. She put her backpack on and got moving, still looking around a little, just waiting for something else to happen. She was so focused on what was behind her and on her sides that she almost walked into someone. It was Steven Richards.

"Hey," he said. "I saw that, and that was really crappy."

Harper was surprised. She did a quick listen to see if it was a trick. He was being genuine. It was based in a hatred of most of their classmates, but it was genuine. "Thanks," she said, "but at this point in my life, I probably should know enough to watch out for packs of running morons in school."

Steven nodded. He might have smiled a little but it was tough to tell. "Yeah, well nobody should have to be on the lookout for stupid their whole life. Except maybe whoever recruits football players."

Harper smiled at him. "You seem like you're in a good mood. I mean, a good mood for you."

He shrugged. "Things could be worse, I guess."

Harper laughed. "That would look great on a bumper sticker or a t-shirt."

Steven looked away. Harper listened in again. He was thinking about the two of them being together, but the way that he was thinking about it made Harper feel gross. He looked back at her. Harper tried to not let her face show that she knew what he'd thought. "Want me to walk with you? To keep you safe?"

Harper would have laughed at that if it had been funny instead of just awful. "No, thanks," she said. "I can watch out for morons myself." She realized, after she'd said it, that she'd probably hurt his feelings. It was ridiculous that she should have to worry about his feelings, but he was important to all this, for some reason, so Harper said, "I mean, I wouldn't mind the company, just don't feel like you have to."

He shrugged again. It seemed to be his go-to move, which seemed appropriate. "Whatever," he said. "If not then I'll just slip in with the cheerleaders and jocks. They all love me."

"I just meant that I'm not an invalid. You don't need to watch out for the girl with CP." After he stared blankly for a few seconds, Harper said, "Cerebral palsy. The thing I have." She held both of her hands out in front of her. He looked at her left hand first, then her right one.

After a few seconds, Steven said, "Huh." Harper resisted the urge to listen to his thoughts. She knew that, if she did, she'd just might hear something that would make her angry. Steven looked away again. He said, "Well, I don't spend more time in school than I have to, so if you want to walk with me, you need to move."

Harper kept herself from smiling as she shrugged. "I guess I could get going."

There was a little change in Steven's face, but Harper caught it. He seemed to notice the shrug joke. "The cheerleaders and jocks are going to be disappointed," he said.

Harper started walking, keeping a bit of distance from Steven without making it too obvious. "So," she said, "what have you been coloring on today?"

"Anything I come across," he said. "I put a stick figure puking on the bottom of my lunch tray."

Harper chuckled. "Well that's appropriate. At least it wasn't the old egg patty today."

"Yeah," he said, "the grilled cheese and tomato soup is actually kind of edible, right?"

"I only ever take cold lunch," Harper said. After a second, she wondered if that made her sound stuck up. "I hate waiting in line," she added.

Steven looked straight ahead, not turning towards Harper when he spoke. "If I didn't have to, I'd definitely avoid standing with all the drones and zombies in line."

"Not that you're wrong," Harper said, "but why do you hate everyone so much?"

They reached the front doors. Steven opened them for Harper. She thanked him and went out. When they'd made it a bit away from the school, he said, "I don't know, to be honest. When I'm at home and just sketching or something, it doesn't seem like such a big deal, but the second that I walk through those doors, it's like someone's flipped a switch and I'm super pissed about everything. Like I see someone, and I'm hating them even before they say anything to me." They kept walking for a bit, then he said, "I guess that I must sound like a real psycho or something, huh?"

For a few seconds, Harper felt like telling him everything, telling him that it wasn't his fault and that all it meant was that he was going to an awful school. But it passed. She didn't want to sound like a psycho herself. So instead, she just said, "I've heard people say a lot crazier things."

"Yeah, well," Steven said, "thanks. But I still could be crazy."

Harper laughed, "Yeah, you could be." She saw her mom's car. Harper stopped before they got too close.

"What if you could do something about those feelings?" Harper asked him.

Steven looked around, then he shrugged, "What, like some kind of therapy or something?"

"No," Harper said. "More like an afterschool club to promote morale and reduce anxiety."

Steven gave a single, harsh laugh. "So, what, like the holding hands club?"

"More like the having the guts and brains to actually do something. But if you're not up to it..."

Steven nodded and raised his eyebrows. "Yeah, because I'm stupid enough to be manipulated that easily. I'm not participating in some church thing."

Harper smiled and sounded pleasant. "Yeah, because getting you to do something that would make your life better is totally manipulating you.

You busted us!"

Steven looked away again. "Well, if you ever have food at your meetings, let me know. Maybe I'll come."

Harper said, "Sure. We'll make sure to have placemats for you to color, too." Harper walked off before he could respond. She made her way towards her mother. She was nearly there when a car rushed by her, going faster than it should have for a high school parking lot. Harper put her left hand on her chest. She started to turn back to look at Steven, but she stopped herself, not wanting him to see her in a panic again. So instead she just got into her mom's car. She tried to slow her breathing as she buckled in.

"Was it just me?" her mom asked, "or was that driver a real jerk?"

"He was a high school boy, Mom," Harper said. "Probably 95% of them are jerks."

Harper's mom smiled. "Well, I know you won't let them get you down."

Harper gave a little bit of a smile. She didn't say anything out loud. She was thinking that she might want to agree with Krista's timetable after all.

~ * ~

James had texted Harper nearly half an hour ago. He knew that being impatient was also being annoying, but being ignored was quite annoying, too. He tried to remind himself that she had been having difficult times lately. She and Krista usually communicated with each other very effectively, but today they had had a real falling out. Or so it had seemed. James wondered if he had perhaps misread the situation. They had seemed angry with each other, when usually Krista would lash out at James himself, but maybe this would end up being a temporary ruffling of feathers, not anything either real or lasting.

James looked down at his phone. After a few seconds, it vibrated and the little envelope icon appeared. He tapped it. "Yes, Monday we start," it read. James immediately replied "Okay."

He looked down at his left, bottom desk drawer. He was able to open it quickly and easily this time. He reached in and pulled out the map of the school that he'd drawn up. He had put x's by the areas that he expected to be high control areas. The trophy case was obviously one, as was the football field. He also put an x by the library, because the old yearbooks were kept there, and they'd have many images of the "Savage" mascot. He put a question mark by the band room. It was entirely possible that there would be some old photos, uniforms, or other memorabilia that would have the mascot on them. He also put a question mark by the pool, for similar reasons. After that, it got harder to predict. Would one of the history teachers have kept old clippings of pictures from years past? Who used to run the debate team? Had they retired? The possibilities were numerous and unpredictable.

James tried rotating the map. Maybe if he had a different angle or perspective, then he'd be able to see a different pattern. The problem, of course, was that the question marks made any sense of precision impossible. He had to have the question marks resolved and the stars confirmed. It was absolutely possible that some of the stars would prove to be false leads. Ideally, he would want to run trials several days in several places, but he knew that he didn't have that luxury. All that they could do was to collect what data they could and hope for a reasonable margin of error.

James looked back at his cell phone. He realized that "Okay" was probably not a sufficient response to Harper, but now that time had passed, he wasn't sure if adding anything would make much sense. He appreciated that the recent lunch chats were task-oriented. Although there was also socialization, the sense of urgency and focus allowed him to have a clear sense of expectations. He wondered, if they were successful, what would happen among the three of them. Would they fall into a state of constant monitoring, always comparing notes to see if the entity was coming back? Or, without the threat of the entity, would Krista and Harper end up dominating the conversation, leaving James in the background? They hadn't discussed a long-term plan at all yet. He tried to recall how it was before the threat. He felt a sense of anxiety about whether or not they would continue to talk to him in the same way if they beat the entity.

James set his phone aside. He picked up his English book. Before he opened it, he quickly looked at his door, making sure that nobody would look in his room. When he saw that no one was there, he closed his eyes. He listened to the sound of the drawer closing. When it had shut entirely, he opened his eyes back up. He opened his book, took out a pencil, and began to read and make notes.

~ * ~

Krista was waiting for Harper near the front doors the next day. Before Harper got close enough to say anything, Krista signed, "Sorry." Harper smiled and pointed at herself, nodding. When Harper got close enough, she told Krista, "James and I are kicking it into high gear today."

Krista smiled. "Look at you two," she said, "ready to kick ass." They walked together without talking for a bit, just enjoying not fighting with each other. They passed by Krista's boy, and he nodded to her. Krista gave a little wave back. When they'd finally passed by, Harper leaned in and asked, "That's him?"

"Don't be reading my mind," she said.

Harper laughed. "He's cute." She touched Krista's elbow, "I hereby give you permission to take the day off of fighting evil so that you can chase boys."

Krista leaned in and spoke quietly. "If I'm chasing him, then I'm doing it wrong."

Harper laughed again. The two of them walked together for a bit longer before parting ways. Krista walked straight, not looking back, Harper veered a bit. She tried to listen in for Krista's boy, to hear if he seemed decent or if he was thinking like Steven was yesterday. But as Harper tried to reach back and catch some of the thoughts, his got lost in the noise and chaos of the hallway. It wasn't that unusual for the mornings, but it still left Harper curious. Then again, maybe staying out of her friend's business would be for the best anyway.

~ * ~

At lunch, they'd agreed on the first step for mapping. Harper and James would eat as quickly as they could. When they'd finished, Harper would go first, seeming to head to the bathroom. She moved a bit slower and usually got a little leeway from the monitors and teachers. A minute or two later, James would head out as well. They'd meet by the trophy case, where James would play the recording while Harper would listen to people's thoughts. Krista had volunteered to be the one to play the recording, since she could turn invisible, but the other two said that James would use his phone and that he could stay out of sight and use his power to turn the phone on and off. When Harper and James had both agreed on this, Krista had just shrugged.

Krista watched her friends go, first Harper with a quick check in with one of the monitors, then James, who just kind of wandered off in his own Jamesy way, not getting stopped mainly because he didn't ask, and the monitors didn't want to deal with the headache. There was something admirable about that.

Krista looked around the lunch hall. She tried not to let herself feel either alone or scared, but it was definitely weird without the other two. With the weirdness at home and the newness of some boy being interested in her, she appreciated the stability that James and Harper gave her. Not that she would ever say that to them. Not only would she feel weird, but she was pretty sure that James's head would start on fire if he heard her or Harper open up to him like that.

Krista let herself look over at Jenna's table. She clapped her hand over her mouth to keep from laughing. Jenna had the blankest look on her face that Krista had ever seen. After that, though, Krista did a sweep of the table and saw something that freaked her out. Although Jenna's little flunkies were all eating different things, they were taking bites and chewing in perfect unison. Krista looked down at the table, not wanting to be noticed by them. She looked down at her lunch. A hot dog, tater tots, green beans and pears. She was sure that all of the flunkies had organic vegetables, fine chocolates and gourmet meats and cheeses.

This made her curious, though, about this whole mapping project. If it was the Savage mascot that gave whatever this was its power, then why did there always seem to be kids under its control in the lunch hall? Krista looked around trying to see if there was some sign. A first look at the room didn't show anything. The second time, she didn't see any Savage mascot, but when she saw the current one, something clicked. When they changed mascots, she was sure that they had just painted over the original. Why would they scrape it off? So, underneath that stupid, growl-faced mascot had to be an offensive and stupid image of a Savage. Krista smiled. She took a couple of tater tots and popped them in her mouth. But when she looked down from the mascot, the smile left her face. All of the flunkies were looking right at her. Krista's mouth went dry. She tried to chew, but the tater tots felt like plastic. Even more than usual.

Getting up and walking off didn't seem like an option. Even if the monitors let her go, she'd be bringing the flunkies right to James and Harper. She could blow the whole operation. Maybe she could head to the bathroom and turn invisible. Krista was still thinking of her options when the flunkies got up, all in unison, and started towards her. Krista swallowed the lump of tater tot that was in her mouth. She didn't think that the thing would have these girls attack her physically. It would send someone else if it was going to do that. Someone stronger. This was just about threatening, and if she remembered that, she would probably be okay. Of course, if scaring her was the goal, it would probably work. She looked straight at them and smiled a convincing smile. She could've been a local meteorologist.

They got to her table and just stood there for a few seconds. Krista took a quick look at Jenna, who still looked exceptionally vacant. One of the flunkies (it didn't matter which) spoke, but Krista missed most of it. She looked back at them and said, "I'm sorry, I missed what you said,"

They all leaned in, and one of the middle ones spoke. "I said, why are you all alone, loser?"

"Alone," Krista said. "With you lovely people here, how could I possibly feel alone?"

Another one, one of the end ones, said, "Nice try, but Freak and Stumbles snuck off somewhere and we want to know what they're trying."

Krista said, "Well, Harper went to the bathroom, but I think that she eats enough fiber that she won't just be trying." After saying it, Krista thought, "Help."

"And Freak?" another one said. "Is he having a splat attack in the bathroom, too?"

Krista shrugged. "Beats me. It's not like I'm his mom or something."

They started to spread out, and Krista recognized right away that some of them were trying to get behind her. She wasn't sure if they had figured out that she was particularly vulnerable from behind or if this was just a normal tactic of horrible and aggressive spirits. Either way, Krista started sliding back.

"Are you his girlfriend?" one of the girls asked.

"Nah," Krista said, "but I can put in a good word for you if you want."

The first one spoke again. "Go ahead and keep talking. We'll surround you while you think you're stalling, then we'll close in and none of the stupid monitors will do a thing. We're in control."

Krista kept smiling and thought "help" again. If they were trying to stop her from stalling, then it probably meant that the stalling was working. "Okay," she said. "I'll tell, just don't attack me."

"You're lying," another one said. "Don't think that we can't tell that you're lying."

"You got me," Krista said. "I was going to lie and tell you that they were baking a special cake for you guys, but that's just smart aleck talk." She stood and started to back away, making sure that she wasn't the center of a circle. "But if I have to tell the truth, then okay. They aren't baking you any cake." She took two steps back. "It's actually a pie."

They started to advance, all stone faced but angry. But, two steps in, they slowed down, then they stopped, their faces as blank as Jenna's. "So," Krista said, "We're all okay with pie, then?"

Krista looked around the lunch hall. Her first observation was that nobody seemed to notice that a group of popular kids who had been looking to beat up a loser girl were all staring off into space now. On a second look, she recognized that Harper must have heard her thoughts. James had come back to the lunch hall. He was standing a couple tables away from the flunkies, and his phone was in his hand. Krista's mind didn't let everything click right away; she was just grateful that the flunkies had been stopped. But she did realize that she didn't have long before a monitor would come over and tell James to put his phone away. So, Krista gave James a quick nod, then she picked up her lunch tray and went to the return area. She dumped everything, thought, "Thanks, Harper," and turned around. It looked like the flunkies were starting to come back to themselves. Not like themselves under control, but their actual selves, trickling back to Jenna's table. Krista ducked out of the lunch hall, heading for the bathroom. Considering the fact that she'd only almost got her ass kicked, things had turned out well. She thought to Harper, "Let's all meet after school."

~ * ~

Harper's mom had given the three of them a ride to the library. The ride had been awkward. Without the topic of the thing in the school, the three of them didn't have a clear topic of conversation. Harper's mom would give little comments or questions, but no real conversation developed. James started explaining the principles of endothermic reactions, and everyone else in the car sat in a bored but grateful silence. When she dropped them off, Harper's mom told the three of them that she'd quickly run to the store to pick up a few things, giving them about half an hour.

The three of them immediately went to the group study area. Krista told them what she'd realized about the mascot in the lunch hall. "Of course," James said. "There are probably old symbols and mascots all over the school. They could be in every classroom, every bathroom. It could be in the walls like asbestos."

"Great," Harper said, "So we just have to have a bake sale and raise money to build a new school."

"We could always just rent one of those wrecking ball cranes and level the place," Krista said.

James said, "While those ideas are both ridiculous, they do highlight the fundamental problem. My map is not going to be enough. We need to take an even bigger picture approach."

"Like what?" Krista said, "You're going to repaint the whole school with anti-evil latex?"

"That's not quite what I had in mind," James said, "but a whole school approach, yes."

"If we try to play the recording, we'll need a constant power source," Harper said.

"That was my first thought," James said. "But as I've been thinking about it, my position has changed."

"Now you're actually *for* evil spirits running the school?" Krista asked.

"Your comments are not helpful," James said. Harper stifled a laugh.

Krista opened her mouth, but she paused, and then said, "Sorry, James. I know you're helping us. Go on."

James stared at her for a second, pondering whether or not she meant it. After concluding that it didn't matter at the present moment, he went on. "What if all of the old signs aren't the generator? What if they're more like a rechargeable battery, where they absorb a kind of hostile energy from everyone?"

"That's kind of terrifying?" Harper said, "because it means that the students are the problem."

"To an extent, yes," James said. "But it also means that if we could cut off the supply to the battery, then it won't be able to charge, implying that even a temporary disruption could be productive."

"So we should go forward, like I said in the first place," Krista said.

James thought about it before responding. "I'll give you partial credit." He leaned forward and spoke a bit softer, but slowly. "We can start soon, but we need some kind of monitoring in place so that we can determine whether or not my hypothesis is correct. We need to see if not only does the entity stop, but the students become more calm and rational."

Krista smiled. "Calm, rational teenagers?"

"So I should wander the school and listen to everyone?" Harper asked.

James said, "That's part of it, for sure. But we really should be watching broadly, thinking about Krista's mother, for instance. And we should be watching out for other problems popping up."

"Great," Krista said, "I'll set up a mani-pedi session with my mom. We can have mother-daughter time so that I can get a sense of if she's evil crazy or plain crazy."

"It doesn't have to be like that," Harper said. "I can ask my mom to give you a ride home today and I can take a baseline reading, then I can take another one after we start things."

"A baseline reading," Krista said.

She looked over at one of the bookshelves. Harper looked over at the librarian. She didn't seem to be watching them, but after the day they made the recording, it seemed like they'd be on her radar. She recognized that this was different for Krista than it would have been for either her or James. Krista's mom was both a problem and a source of consistency. And they were treating her like an experiment. Krista might talk crap about her mom, but they were family.

"I just want to know how it's affecting things across town. We didn't want to defeat it in the school only to have it get stronger somewhere else." James said.

Krista sighed. "But if your theory is correct, James, then when we shut it down for a while, then my mom might actually turn normal after the charge is gone,"

"I think it's possible," James said. "But I should also be fully honest and tell you that each person is very complicated, so there's no telling what could end up happening."

Krista looked at James, who looked at the table, she said, "So she could end up being even crazier or she could beat me or something else."

"As I said," James said, "I should be honest, and if I am to be honest, then I have to tell you that, yes, any outcome is possible." He looked at Krista briefly, then looked down again and continued. "But I also think that she'll be more predictable and less prone to aggression."

There was a bit of quiet, then Krista said, "Well, what fun would life be if we didn't roll the dice on our own personal safety sometimes, right?"

The three of them hashed out the rest of their plan before Harper's mom came to pick them up. James had called his parents, and his father picked him up. Harper's mom gave Krista a ride home, just as planned. Krista's mom was even home, and Harper took a listen, briefly, but long enough. It wasn't like Brent's mind, but it was there, just low-key.

~ * ~

Krista knew that Harper and James would have been texting most of the weekend. Probably they didn't totally change the plan, but they were bound to have made little adjustments. Whatever they did, Krista still had to serve detention that night, so her part was pretty limited. When she got to school, Krista looked around for Harper. It took about ten minutes of wandering the halls before Krista saw her. She made her way over to Harper, but she didn't greet her. Harper didn't either. She did, though, hand Krista a sheet of paper folded into a small square. Harper took it and walked away. She looked around, nobody was watching, but she went to her locker anyway. She opened the locker and pretended to rummage around a little, actually unfolding the note and reading it twice. She could pretty much work out what Harper and James must have texted each other from the small changes they'd made to the plan. This would put her home a little bit later than she'd expected, but it wouldn't be that big of a deal. In fact, she might need the extra time to prepare herself for seeing her mother. Krista refolded the note and put it in her back pocket. Then, she took out a couple of books and closed her locker.

~ * ~

In everyone's first hour, they talked a bit about how Tommy would be back the next day. There was some discussion of how he should be treated, that he would be different now and would need some support. Although the three of them weren't together, Harper, Krista, and James all had similar reactions. If the school had created an environment that was welcoming for disabled students, they wouldn't need a conversation like this in the first place. Of course, none of them said anything in the moment. It would have served no purpose in that moment.

At lunch, none of the three of them spoke directly of the plan. James asked Krista if she'd gotten the note from Harper, and she'd replied with a single, slow nod. Then, they were quiet for a bit. "How is the lunch today, Krista?" James asked after a while.

"Same as usual, basically crappy, but at least free for me," Krista said.

"Well," James said, "I suppose that it could be worse." Krista smiled at him.

"What?" James asked, looking first at Krista, then at Harper.

"Nothing," Krista said. "I just appreciate the optimism today."

"I'm going to believe that this is earnest rather than sarcastic." James said.

Krista said, "That's a good assumption, James."

Harper was the first one to notice Jenna. Harper jumped a little when she first saw her. Jenna just smirked as the other two started to turn towards her, "What's up, dorks?" she said.

Krista smiled, "We were just waiting for one of the cool kids to come over and grace us with the glory of their presence. Lucky us, it's you."

"That's funny, loser," Jenna said. "I mean, it's not, but I'm being polite."

Harper laughed, "That's you being polite, huh?"

Jenna waved a hand. "Whatever," she said. "I just came over because my good friends over there told me that one of you really creeped them out the other day."

James said "They probably initiated the encounter. If they just leave us alone, then I'm sure they'll be fine. They do have you after all."

Jenna made a face at James. "Just leave them alone, or I'll go talk to the principal and some of the teachers about how you've been harassing us."

Harper raised her eyebrows. "And if we tell them about how you mocked my disability?"

Jenna scrunched up her face. "What are you talking about, weirdo?"

Harper let herself smirk just a little. "Jenna, if I tell a teacher that you walked over to our table, looked me in the eye, and called me an ugly gimp, it would be no less true than any garbage story that you tell someone about us bothering your airhead friends."

"More true," said James, "since she has two witnesses."

Krista said, "And they'll be on high alert for people bullying disabled students with Tommy due to come back soon."

Jenna turned away, saying, "Whatever."

James called her name. She turned back and raised her eyebrows, not saying anything. James said, "You look nice today." The specifics of what went through Jenna's mind were unclear, but what her face showed was first revulsion, then confusion, then rage. She turned again and headed back towards her table. Krista put her head down and laughed quietly but with big shakes. When she raised her head again, she gave James a high five, which he took with good humor and without leaving Krista hanging.

~ * ~

The rest of the day was mainly uneventful. All three of them felt a little like they were being watched, but it was hard to know if the feeling was legitimate or just a matter of nerves. Harper had difficulty focusing in class, missing chunks of the lecture. Krista knew that she'd blown a pop quiz in social studies. James threw himself into taking notes and completing worksheets. By the end of the day, all three of them were a mixture of keyed up and exhausted, but they had a sense of resolve.

Krista went to the lunch hall for detention. She had all of her things and the little "disruptors" that James had given her at the end of lunch. He'd marked a red line on the volume dial so that she didn't have to worry about setting it. Krista sat at a table and looked around. There was the riffraff that she'd expected: that one weirdo who'd gotten in trouble for stealing one of the dead frogs from the biology lab, that poor, heavy-set girl that anyone could get to yell curse words with about three minutes of teasing, that red-headed kid that never seemed to be out of trouble. But then, two tables over, was Krista's boy. For a second, Krista couldn't breathe. She looked down at her table and told herself to relax. It didn't change anything with respect to the plan. Even now, Harper and James would be laying other disruptors around the school, and, after her own contribution, she would walk home (maybe accompanied by the boy), and observe her mother's behavior, deciding if she needed a disruptor in her own home. It would still be a simple operation. James had told Krista that they needed her to place them after detention because that would give the entity the least amount of time to find the disruptors, but Krista knew that was a lie. They just wanted her to feel like she was doing something. Krista resented that a little at first, but she got over it quickly enough.

After a few minutes, Mr. Hamilton stood up and gave the rules. Krista watched him speak. He mumbled a little, but Krista was pretty sure that he told them that they could do homework quietly, but no phones. When he finished, Krista took out some math homework. She had a hard time focusing. There was a string of word problems with a mix of numbers you needed and ones you didn't. Krista tried to get the first one done. She knew she screwed up because the answer was a really long decimal, so she erased it and started over. The second time, she got 7 as the answer. It seemed like that could be the answer.

Krista looked around. About a third of the students were asleep or had their heads down. Most of the rest were staring off into space or drawing on themselves or their books. Her boy was looking right at her. Krista froze for a second, then she smiled and gave a little wave. He smiled and gave a little nod. Krista tried not to blush. She looked back down at her math problems. It was even harder to get any focus now. If things worked out today, maybe she could try going out with this guy. It would be a good excuse to be out of the house and away from her mother while she was potentially more dangerous.

As the time wound down, Krista put her homework away. She'd gotten it down to one problem. Krista packed things into her bag and kept her disruptor at the very top. She had a hand on one, but not too hard. James had probably spent a lot of time on these things, and Krista knew that fixing one would be out of her ability. She kept her eyes on her bag, not wanting to make eye contact with her boy. While it would be kind of nice to give another wave, she needed to drop the disruptors somewhere where nobody would see it, and she was sure that he wouldn't want to hang out in the lunch hall and then briefly close his eyes for no reason. Krista decided that she would rush out but leave something in the lunch hall so that she could come back and drop one disruptor behind the soda machine and a couple more behind tables that almost never got moved. It never got stocked anymore, but nobody had bothered to take it out of the lunch hall, either. It was the perfect place for something small to be as invisible as Krista herself.

Krista jumped a little. Everyone was starting to move. She must have missed Mr. Hamilton telling them that it was time to go. Krista gathered up her things, but by the time she was up, her boy was almost right next to her already. She slipped two of the disruptors in her pocket and stood up. He walked up to her and smiled. "Hey," he said. "Do you want to see something cool?"

Krista wondered what would qualify as "cool." She didn't want to be a jerk, but she also didn't want to press her luck by wandering around the school until they got kicked out of school before she had a chance to place the disruptor. "Where is it?" she asked.

"Just down the hall," he said, pointing, "Only take a minute or two."

Krista tried to figure out what she could leave to come back for later. "Yeah," she said, "Sure, I like to look at stuff that's cool." She slung her backpack over one shoulder and looked back at Mr. Hamilton. He was looking down at his phone and gathering up his own things. When Krista turned back to her boy, he was smiling.

"You'll like this," he said.

He took her by the arm. It wasn't hard, but it still annoyed Krista a little. Still, she followed along until they got to the hallway, then she stopped and said, "Just a second." She tossed her backpack by the soda machine. He looked at her and Krista shrugged. "Do I need it?"

He shrugged back. "I guess not."

They went on a bit, then stopped in front of the janitor's closet. Krista raised an eyebrow and the boy laughed. "It's not what you think." After a pause, he added, "I promise."

"All right," Krista said, "but I'm not sniffing paint fumes or anything like that, either,"

The boy gave a quiet laugh and shook his head. He stood between Krista and the door for a second, his back to Krista. She figured that he must have picked the lock, because he opened the door. He extended an arm, like someone doing a bad impression of a gentleman. Krista could feel her heart start to pound. Still, she went in. She looked around a little, but it didn't look like anything but cleaning supplies. She turned around to see the boy closing the door. When he looked at her, Krista felt like she'd been punched in the gut. "I don't know exactly what you're trying, but it won't work."

Krista stepped back. She stumbled over something but didn't fall all the way. "This isn't you," she said.

He smiled. "This is all of us. This is our school." He grabbed some duct tape off of one of the shelves. He moved forward, peeling some of the tape off. "I don't have to kill you. I mean, I could, after I get you tied up here. I'm sure there's something I could use in here."

Krista reached into her pocket, touching her disruptor. James hadn't said how it worked, because he was supposed to do the actual turning on tomorrow during school. He'd only said that he'd use his power to turn them on, but that must mean that there was a button or switch. Krista didn't want to take it out if the boy could be the eyes and ears of the thing running the school. She ran her hand along the disruptor, trying to find something. "What do you want with the school, anyway? What are you trying to do?"

The boy shook his head. "I told you, it's what you want. It's what you all want."

Krista moved again, this time to the side. "And that is?"

The boy peeled off a little more tape. "To eat each other, basically. To pull each other down." He got close to her. "I wouldn't do anything you all didn't want me to on some level."

Krista turned the disruptor in her pocket. She'd covered half of it without finding a switch. "So if I tell you I don't want to be tied up in the janitor's closet, you'll let me go?"

The boy laughed. "That's not how it works. You all ask me in a much more subtle way. You usually don't realize what you're asking. Sometimes you don't even know *that* you're asking."

Krista felt it. There was a small, hard bit poking out one of the sides. She gently tried to push it down, but it wouldn't move. "So it's like we're praying in our sleep?"

He laughed again. "I like you. You're funny and you're smarter than you think you are." The boy touched her arm, pulling her closer. "You could serve the school well."

"Wait," Krista said. "I get it. You're going to tie me up and use my being missing to freak out Harper and James. But first, I need to know, this boy that you're in right now. Was all of this a trick to have something on me, or did he actually like me at some point?"

The boy blinked. "As I said, I can't do things that people don't want on some level."

Krista pushed on the switch, down this time instead of up. The switch slid. "That's what I thought," she said.

It didn't happen right away. At first, the boy's grip tightened on Krista's arm, but then it loosened, and his eyes went a little out of focus. Krista kneed him in the groin, twice. The boy doubled over, and Krista shoved him to the ground. She headed for the door. Krista closed the door behind her. She ran to the lunch hall to grab her bag and leave the disruptor. Most of the kids had gone, but Mr. Hamilton was still there. He looked up at Krista. She couldn't tell if he was himself or working for the thing running the school. She knew that she shouldn't trust him to protect her if the boy came back out, and he would come out eventually. Krista went to her bag. She turned the disruptor off and put it in her pocket, still watching Mr. Hamilton. He was just kind of staring at her. Maybe he was still in the fog before he came out of the thing's control. She'd have to work fast.

Krista yelled, "Forgot my backpack," probably a little too loudly. She grabbed her backpack with her left hand, and with her right, she slid another disruptor behind the backpack. She'd shoved it hard enough that it went under the soda machine. She stood and slung her backpack over her shoulder. "Sorry, I'll be gone now," she said, and she turned around quickly. "Oh hey," she said, "a quarter!" She went to one of the folded-up tables and slid another disruptor underneath it. She kept moving and tried not to look at Mr. Hamilton. If her back was to him, then she could at least claim to not hear anything if he called her name.

Krista left the lunch hall and turned away from the main doors. It would make the way to an exit longer, but it also would mean that she'd be less likely to see the boy. The problem was that she was already starting to get out of breath. She knew, though, that she couldn't stop, so she ran on, slowing down a little with each step. She made it out the door. In front of her was the football field and some woods. She did a quick look around. She was alone. Krista put her backpack under her jacket and turned invisible. She knew that anyone under the thing's control could still tell that she was around, but maybe wouldn't be able to know exactly where.

Krista decided to head for the woods. It seemed like the thing would believe that she had escaped, but escaped without doing what she was supposed to do. She got to the first set of trees. Looking back to see that she wasn't being followed yet. She collapsed behind the largest tree and caught her breath. She tried to breathe quietly, but she knew that she didn't have a good sense of if she was doing it or not. After she slowed her breathing a bit, she looked out from behind the tree. Her boy had come out of the school. He was walking funny, which Krista was glad to see. It looked like he was headed towards the football field. Krista slowly moved back behind the tree. She knew that probably the next hour was going to be hell. She wouldn't know for sure when it was safe to move.

On top of that was the fact that it wasn't going to get any warmer. She'd be stuck trying to watch for shadows and movement until she couldn't stand it anymore. Then, assuming that she got home safely, her mother would almost certainly be working for the thing running the school. Would Krista's boy know to head to her house? Maybe he was already there. Maybe they were deciding what to use to tie her up with. That made Krista wonder, what would the boy remember from the closet? Would he only remember her kneeing him and shoving him to the ground? Why would he think that he'd brought her to the closet in the first place? Or would he have forgotten it all?

Krista thought she saw something moving. She pushed herself back into the tree as far as she could. It wasn't her boy. It was a rabbit. Krista wondered if the thing running the school could control animals. It didn't seem any less realistic than there being a thing running the school in the first place. At first, Krista did think the thing was controlling the rabbit. It seemed to look in her general direction.

She thought about how to kill the rabbit. She pictured herself picking up a rock and tossing it, but, on some level, she knew that was ridiculous. The thing in the school was probably laughing right now, probably sending the whole football team. Krista put a hand over her mouth and tried not to sob. But then the rabbit hunkered down, and she realized what it was doing. The rabbit was trying to find the thing that it could smell but not see. Krista realized that she was safe.

She waited a bit longer. The rabbit sniffed one last time, then hopped away. Krista stood slowly, trying to be as quiet as she could. Her legs had grown stiff. She bent and extended each one. After she felt a little looser, she looked out from behind the tree. The boy wasn't anywhere that Krista could see. That didn't mean he wasn't there. Krista stayed invisible. Even if he could see her, maybe the invisibility would give her the extra step she'd need to get away. She started to head home, but she remembered that she couldn't trust it to be safe there. So she stood there, invisible and alone, thinking about her options. Eventually, she turned and headed in a different direction.

~ * ~

James's immediate reaction was panic. He had no clue who would be there to see him. Would the entity be bold enough to come to his front door? If it was, then how did it know that it needed to stop them now? He thought that they'd been careful. James's mother, the one who'd told him someone was asking for him, was still standing in the door to his room. James said, "Tell them that I'll be down in just a second."

That seemed to satisfy his mother. She turned and went. James opened his desk drawer and took out a spare disruptor. He slid it into his pocket and kept a hand on the switch. He wished that he'd paid closer attention to his mother's tone and facial expression to get a sense of the level of threat that he should be expecting. Then again, she might not recognize whatever the entity had sent as a genuine threat. Or maybe the entity could influence her. Was there any memorabilia in their home?

By the time that he reached the bottom of the steps, his heart was pounding. When he saw Krista at his front door, he froze. His first assumption was that she had come by to report on the success or failure of her part of the placements. Looking at her a bit more carefully, he recognized that there was something else entirely. She looked exhausted. "Hello," he said, "are you okay?"

Krista looked at James's mother, then back at him. "Yeah," she said. "I'm fine. I was just wondering if I could ask something, though. About our project." Then, she glared at James's mother again.

James nodded, not sure what was coming next. "If I can help you, then I definitely will." He tried to think of what classes he and Krista might have in common. Did she need help with a math worksheet?

"You know the project that you and Harper were working on today?"

James nodded. "The mascot project?" he asked.

Krista smiled. "Yes," she said. "I was wondering if what you made would last the night if I needed to use it in my home tonight."

"At home?" James took a quick look at his mother and then looked back to Krista. Neither one seemed particularly happy, and James had no idea how to negotiate the situation.

"Yeah," Krista said, "Will it last the whole night?"

"I believe that would be fine," James said.

Krista smiled. "Awesome. Well, I really do appreciate it."

"And you know how to work it?" James asked.

Krista was quiet for a moment, then she said, "Yeah, I've got it." She looked at James's mother one last time, "and sorry for bothering you in the evening."

"No bother," James's mother said, "I'm always happy to meet one of James's friends."

Krista nodded, then turned and left. James's mother closed the door. She turned to James and asked "You're working on a project for the school's mascot?"

James had skipped telling his mother things before, but he wasn't used to lying to her outright. "Project is probably too formal of a description. It's just something a friend asked for help with." He stood still, not sure if that would be sufficient or if his mother would have a follow up.

"But you built something for this project?"

James had no idea how to avoid answering the question. "One of my classmates and I designed something. It really doesn't do much, but my classmate seemed to be interested in it."

"The classmate you worked with or the one that just came to the door."

"Both, I suppose." James began slowly moving towards the stairs.

"Did you ever think that maybe one of them is more interested in you than in the device?"

James stopped moving. "I would prefer that the conversation stops here."

His mother shrugged. "Okay, James, but sooner or later, you'll have to confront the possibility that a girl, or even more than one girl, could find you attractive."

James thought about this for a few seconds. There was so much that he couldn't tell his mother. He really didn't want to, other than to let her know that she was wrong in this case. All he said to his mother was, "I'll take that into consideration," and then he went up to his room. He went in, closed the door, and took out his phone. He knew that he should text Harper, but he was unsure of what to say. He wasn't entirely sure of what Krista's visit meant. It didn't look like she'd been assaulted, but he'd been so surprised to see her that maybe he'd missed the evidence. In the end, he sent three sentences. "Krista stopped by. Seemed OK. Should meet her outside school tomorrow."

He set the phone aside and just sat, going over the possibilities in his head. When his phone vibrated, he picked it up. Harper had sent an emoji with a concerned look on its face. James texted back, "I agree." Then, he set his phone aside and laid down on his bed.

~ * ~

James had arrived first, then Harper. He was grateful that his mother didn't see a girl waiting for him outside of school. Things were strange enough with the odd coincidence of it being Tommy's first day back at school after the accident. Ella had greeted Tommy at the front door. She'd had a "welcome back" card and different candies for Tommy. He seemed unimpressed. Or maybe he was just suffering from the anxiety of being back after so long. Or of having to return to school in a wheelchair.

Harper got to school while Ella was giving Tommy his gifts. Harper and James watched together, but silently. Krista got there last and not long before school started. She kept looking around. Harper waved her over. "Are you okay?" she asked.

Krista told them about being attacked, and she tried to explain about the rabbit. It didn't go well.

"I don't think the entity perceives smell any more than we do," James said.

"No," Krista said. "I mean that it's not that they can see me even when I'm invisible, it's that they can pick up on where I am because it's connected to every student in the school."

"Every student?" Harper said. "You mean it tries to control every student?"

"Yeah," Krista said, "but we influence it, too. It does what the students ask it to."

James looked at the ground. "So we could just ask it to stop and it would?"

"No," Krista said. "The whole student body has to ask. But we don't do it directly. We don't know that we're doing it."

"How do you know this?" Harper asked.

Krista could feel her cheeks go red. "You know my boy?"

"What boy?" James said.

"Yeah," Harper said. "How would he know?"

"Yesterday," Krista said. "He was under its control. He was the one tried to tie me up in the janitor's closet after detention, and he, like, talked to me."

"We need to turn him in," James said.

"To who, James?" Harper said, then to Krista, "God, are you okay?"

"I'm fine," Krista said. "Look, we need to go in before the bell rings."

"I still say we need to do something," James said. "We can't just let him go."

"It wasn't him," Krista said. "I mean, it was, but it was all of us."

"What does that mean?" James asked.

Krista shook her head. "Just, let's go inside. I think I'm done talking about it. Go ahead with your plan today, and we can talk about it after school. I don't want to think about it." Neither James nor Harper tried to stop her as Krista went in. They both stood outside quiet for a moment. "Did she tell you anything about this last night?" Harper asked. "Is that what you were texting me about?"

"No," James said. "This is all news to me."

Harper looked around. Any of the kids going into the school could be a threat. All of them could be. In fact, if what Krista said was true, all of them were one big threat.

James said, "Who's her boy?"

Harper said, "It's not a big deal. I mean, I don't know if it is, but…" Harper thought about it. "Don't be jealous," she said, smiling.

"I'm not jealous, I'm just concerned about its potential impact upon our plan...and Krista"

Harper wanted to listen to his thoughts to hear the nature of James's interest. She was genuinely curious, but she didn't want him to lose trust in her. "All right," she said. "Krista's right. We should head in." The two went in without talking. When they parted ways, Harper said, "See you at lunch."

~ * ~

James closed his eyes. Krista assumed that he was doing it, flipping on the switches of all of the disruptors over the entire school. She wondered if their size made it harder or easier for James. Krista looked over at the popular kid table. They all looked angry. They weren't actually doing anything yet. They were just watching, which suggested that they didn't really know what was going on. Krista looked at Harper. She wasn't really looking at anything, she was just staring off into space, so she must have been listening to see if they would be stopped. Krista didn't want to admit to herself that she felt left out, but it was hard not to.

When there was a little more quiet, she looked back at the table, the popular kids were starting to look around. They didn't quite look confused, yet, more like they could hear something quiet and they were trying to figure out what it was and where it came from. Krista looked at another table, this one filled with a bunch of forgettable boys. They'd all stopped eating. In fact, it looked like they'd stopped moving entirely, like someone had managed to stop time. Krista found herself hating the boys. They seemed so weak, frozen there and not doing anything. She could probably climb under her own table, turn invisible, then go to their table and start beating one of them with a lunch tray. Or jabbing them with a fork, though the crappy school forks would probably bend before they did any real damage.

Krista shook her head. She realized that the thing running the school must be scrambling, trying to find anyone to jump into. She looked over at Harper. Tears were coming down her cheeks. Krista reached over and touched her forearm. Harper jumped, startled. She looked over at Krista and laughed. "It's working," she said, "Everyone is starting to get free." She put a hand on Krista's.

"What if," Krista said, "freedom is scary at first?" After a bit of quiet (the lunch hall had become eerily quiet) she added, "What if this thing was less of a jail cell and more of a dam that was holding back everyone's bad emotions. Or maybe just directing them?"

"So you think that we're breaking the dam?" Harper asked.

Krista looked around, then she pointed. Harper and James looked over to see Steven Richards. He was crying. Not just a little, either. He had one of his hands over his mouth, and tears were visible from several tables over. Krista pointed again. This time, it was a lunch monitor. She was bent forward, her hands on her knees. It looked like she might throw up at any moment. Next, she pointed at Jenna's table. They were all glaring at each other, alternating between muttering to each other and not looking at each other. "Looks like bad news to me," Krista said. Suddenly, the lunch monitor that looked like she might throw up actually did throw up. People were going up to Tommy, touching his shoulder, his hand, and the three of them could tell that this would be what people would claim made everyone sad, but they knew better.

"What do you suggest?" James said. "We keep making ourselves vulnerable? We let the entity take over the school again, preying on the weak?"

Krista looked at James for a moment before answering. "No," she said, "I think that we should sit down with it. Talk directly to it."

There was a little more quiet, and then Harper said, "This is a joke, right?"

"No," Krista said. "We tell it that we're in control, and then we let it know that we'll let it exist, but it has to follow certain rules, or we kill it."

"That's ridiculous," James said. "Even if we trusted it, we can't talk to it."

"I did," Krista said, "Through my boy yesterday, it talked directly to me."

The other two were quiet, then James asked, "What exactly did it tell you?"

"It didn't explain everything, but it said that it only acts on what the students want. I think it's like all the worst thoughts and feelings in the school got together and grew a brain."

"So how do we get your boy free without freeing the rest of the school?" James asked.

"We won't have to," Krista said. "You guys will come over to my place after school."

~ * ~

The rest of the day had been hard. Everyone was either weepy or angry. The teachers kept getting distracted or just trailing off. In Chemistry, Mr. Barnes almost set his tie on fire over a Bunsen burner. In PE, two of the football players got into a shoving match and a third one looked on, crying. The sport for the day was badminton. By the end of the day, all of the three were creeped out, even though none of them were the target of any aggression. People weren't really polite, but they were mopey, either saying how sad it was to see Tommy this way (which pissed off Krista, because he was like Alyssa, who was a person, not a tragedy) or saying very teen things like, "I just can't deal today." On the other hand, not being the target for once made it worse.

At the end of the day, the three of them rode with Harper's mother. "So," she asked, "you guys are working on the same project as before, or something new?"

"Same one," Krista said, "but we're really close to done."

"Well, that's good news," Harper's mom said.

"Some of us are less confident of that claim than others," James said.

"Some of us are just negative Nancies," Krista said, smirking.

Harper's mom chuckled quietly. "I'm sure that you three will work it out."

"That's what we're about to do, right?" Harper asked.

Both Krista and James muttered, "Yeah." Harper met her mother's eyes in the rearview mirror. Harper could tell that she was smiling. Harper quickly listened to her mother's thoughts. She was happy that Harper was having just the usual struggles with keeping friends together, not serious struggles like depression or sexual harassment. Harper almost laughed. Not only did her mom not know what she and her friends were facing, she also didn't really know what went on at school.

Harper's mom dropped them off with little fanfare. Krista apologized that her mom wouldn't be able to give Harper a ride home, but Harper's mom said that it was no big deal. James had gotten a number of texts from his mother. He suspected that it was related to Krista's late visit the previous night followed by a notification that he would be late getting home today. They went into Krista's house. Harper had tried listening outside. She didn't pick anything up. When they went in and confirmed that, Krista gave them the full plan. They sat quietly then, for nearly ten minutes. When Krista's mom came in, she looked around, then laughed. "Krista, you having a big party while I'm out?"

"Nah," Krista said, "a school project."

"Good," Krista's mom said. "You could stand to bring your grades up."

"Speaking of school," Krista said, "do you still have your letterman's jacket?"

Krista's mom looked around the room. "What kind of project are you guys working on?"

"Ancient History," Krista said, not cracking a smile.

Krista's mom gave a hint of a smile. "If your brain was as smart as your mouth, then you wouldn't need any help from your friends," she said. Still she turned and went to her room.

"You're sure about this?" Harper asked Krista.

"When have I been sure about anything?" she asked.

"You've been sure that I'm wrong a number of times," James said. Krista and Harper laughed quietly. They went to sit at the kitchen table, and James followed suit. When Krista's mother came back out, she looked angry. She'd already put the jacket on, and they could all tell who was in control. "So," she said, "You're all here to laugh. But you might not be as smart as you think you are. What if I block the door and start the house on fire?"

"You'd kill your last vessel," Harper said, "You couldn't do that."

"It's hardly the entity's last vessel," James said. When Krista and Harper looked at him, he added, "There must be Savage mascots and memorabilia all over town. It could find another place to pop up, but we're not here to shut down Krista's mom anyway."

"Smart boy," Krista's mom said. "Why are you here then?"

Krista said, "We want to call a truce. You know that we can shut you down both in the school and out, and we know that you can still hurt people we care about. Let's call it a draw."

"You might think that you have me beat," Krista's mother said, "but I was part of the school before any of you were born, and I'll be there when you're all dead."

"All the more reason for a truce," James said. "Take a bit of time off while we're here, wait until we're dead." The other two looked at him. "Or just until we graduate, and then take back full control of the school without our interference."

Krista's mother stared at James for a bit. "You don't think like the others do."

"That's a fair assessment," James said. "So you agree with me?"

Krista's mother shook her head. "It would give you far too much time to plot against me. You could set up all kinds of traps and devices around town."

"You wouldn't be out of the school," Harper said. "You'd still be able to see what we're doing, right?"

Now Krista's mother looked at Harper for a bit. "Inside the school and out, yes. Though perhaps a bit less than usual."

"So it would be impossible for us to sneak anything past you, then," Harper said.

"You were just able to chase me out of the school. It seems like that should concern me."

"And we're here talking to you," James said. "We could be

expanding our attack, but instead, we're sitting down to speak with you. Shouldn't that set your mind at ease?"

Krista's mom leaned back in her chair and smiled. "Yes," she said. "Why are you here talking to me instead of attacking? What happened in the school when you shut me down?"

Krista put her hands in the air, like she was surrendering, but she was also smiling. "You busted us, Ma. Once we put you down, everyone in the school started to have these really weird breakdowns. And not always in a fun way, either. Though I bet watching someone's tie catch fire was pretty hilarious."

"It was actually quite upsetting," James said.

"Wait," Harper said, "let's not pretend that you care about the students or teachers. I mean, what you're doing right now is trying to manipulate us into letting you fully loose again."

Krista's mom shrugged. "You know how to read minds; you should be able to answer that yourself."

Harper said, "Even if I got sucked in while trying to read your mind right now, my friends would be able to put a stop to it. We can control you, or stop you, anyway."

"We can stop you," James said, "but we realize now that we would prefer to have something keeping the school in check. Still, we have to set some rules so that we can trust that you won't be a destructive force."

"I told her," Krista's mother said, pointing at Krista, "I do what the students want me to do. If you want the school to be peaceful, then you need to change the students. And good luck with that. You can't imagine some of the things that they've done with my help. The times that groups of you students punched and stomped on others because they thought they were gay."

"We don't need the full list," Harper said, "but you're claiming that you have no influence? That you can't act? We know that that's a lie."

"The time one of you chased a dog around with a taser he'd stolen from a visiting speaker."

"This list only proves that you take pleasure in this history," James said, "just as you've taken pleasure in targeting us."

"I've targeted you," Krista's mother said, "because the students fear change, and they don't like people who are different, people who make them feel uncomfortable. You were all different, in more than one way, and I'll add, you were trying to change the school. You still are, in fact. That's exactly why they hate you."

"So you'll go back to attacking us?" Krista asked. "There's no way we can work with each other?"

Krista's mother sat quietly for some time. "As I said, I act on student desires. Dark desires, at times. Like the group of boys who—"

"That's enough," Krista said. "We get it, you're willing to participate in anything. We're saying we want that to stop, to set some kind of rules."

"You say that you want to give me rules, but what rules will you follow? How will you ease everyone's mind?"

After a moment, James said, "It is a fair question." This was followed by a punch in the arm from Krista.

"Fair?" she said. "You're going to negotiate with something that was going to tape me up and leave me in the janitor's closet just yesterday? That's been harassing all of us basically this whole year?"

Krista's mother said, "Weren't you going to completely destroy me before you saw what happened to the school? We're both only here out of fear and a sense of self-preservation."

"That's not totally true," Harper said. "We're also looking out for other students, some of whom would make fun of us or look down on us even without your influence."

Krista's mother laughed. "You still don't understand what I am. Not really." She looked at each of the three of them before continuing. "I don't influence the kids who pick on you, I reflect their drive to keep holding you down. When you protect them, you work to protect the biggest source of my power."

"The biggest?" James asked "So there are other sources?"

Krista's mother shrugged. "Just as you need both food and oxygen to survive, I'm not so simple as a mirror for angry teenagers. I can honestly say that I never remember a time when I had to go hungry."

"The mascot," Harper said. "Even if you didn't have the students you have the mascot?"

Krista's mother shook her head. "Why do you think this is the mascot? Pure chance? The fear of difference and the need for dominance are built into all of you. I just manage it directly."

"You can manage it, then?" James asked. "You could direct it in a more positive way?"

"I might be able to make the school hate a different group of kids, if that's what you want." Krista's mother said.

"That can't be it," Krista said. "That's just the same thing applied to a different group."

Krista's mother shrugged again. "Then you need to find some way to change what the school wants."

"How do we do that?" James asked.

"That," Krista's mother said, "is not my problem." She crossed her arms and smiled. They all sat that way for a bit, not knowing how to break the stalemate. Eventually, Harper said, "What about this? You work to introduce a sense of calm into the school for one month. During that time, you let me listen to people's minds, and you let us try to influence the school. If we can change things, then you'll continue to keep the peace in the school, reflecting the direction that the school is headed."

"In one month?" Krista's mom asked. "You expect to make a drastic change in a single month? And if you don't then I just go back to things as normal?"

"It won't be a major change," Harper said, "but it will be a change."

Krista's mother repeated herself. "And if you fail, then I go back to things as normal?"

"Or we shut you down again," James said. "If you truly are what you say you are, then you should be fully aware of the mental state of the students, and you'll recognize whether or not we're making progress. If there's even subtle progress, then you'll need to honor our bargain."

"And if you do turn things around," Krista's mother said, "then I'll be a force of good? You'll let me continue on, because you believe that I'll enhance the positive feelings in the school?"

"If you really are a reflection," Krista said, "then you shouldn't care what the school does, you should just reflect it, right? And if it is good, then why should we stop you?"

"You need to understand, it's not just the school. I reflect the school, and the school reflects the town. This task is no small thing and I am not sympathetic to your cause by my nature."

"Honestly," Harper said, "this is something we should have been doing already, even if just for the sake of human decency."

Krista's mother laughed. "Having been here for as long as I have, I find that phrase hilarious."

"We're not laughing," Krista said. "Maybe you've only stayed at the 'whole town' detached level for so long that you don't get individual suffering, but we get it."

Krista's mother turned to James. "Why do this?" You've already demonstrated some level of control over me. Why not use that to dominate the school?"

James raised his eyebrows. "I find it interesting that you assume that I'm susceptible to this type of persuasion. What is your reason for wanting to keep a sense of dominance, anyway?"

Krista's mother smiled. "I told you. I reflect the town, and the town fears change. Deeply."

"This will become normal. It will become a stability, and then the town will fear anything else."

Krista's mom studied Harper before replying. "You really do believe that. Interesting. Well, there's still the matter of this calm that you suggested. How do you expect me to accomplish that?"

"I've been thinking about that," Harper said. "To be honest, I expected that getting you under control would bring this big sense of calm, but obviously that was wrong."

"How did you put me under some kind of control, anyway?" Krista's mom asked.

Immediately, Krista said, "There's this weird little caterpillar that emits a strange but subtle odor. We found it as part of this project that we're doing on butterflies, and we realized that it can disrupt your control over people, so we put little cocoons all around the school. Soon, they'll become butterflies, flying through the school and disrupting your control even more intensely; then they'll lay eggs, and you'll really be in trouble."

Krista's mother nodded. "You're quite an impressive liar. Were it not for your friend's expressions, I would have had to consider it whether or not you were lying."

Krista said, "I was once voted 'Most Likely to Become a Politician.'"

"Don't you have to be diplomatic to be a politician?" James asked. Krista laughed.

"So you're not going to tell me how you shut me down?" Krista's mother asked. She was smiling.

"I'm a bit surprised that you don't know," Harper said. "You can't access our thoughts?"

"To a degree," Krista's mother said. "With many students, I can see or hear exactly what they think. They give to me everything. With the three of you, and with a small number of others, it's more like listening to a conversation through a door. I can get a sense of what's going on, but I miss the specifics. But this is getting me nowhere, so let's get back to the topic of calm."

"As you wish," Harper said. "Right now, it's aggression that makes people feel comfortable and powerful, right?"

"That's generally true," Krista's mother said, "though I certainly don't make those rules."

"So," James said, "a common enemy might let everyone feel in power and comfortable together."

"True," Harper said, "but that still relies on anger or fear. A common friend wouldn't."

"Holy crap," Krista said. "How are you going to find a friend of Jenna's and Steven's?"

"It does seem improbable," James said.

"It does," Harper said, "But so does the idea of some horrible force running our school, right?"

"I'm only as horrible as the people I reflect."

"That's fair," Krista said. When the other two looked at her she shrugged and said, "What? It is."

"Fair or not," Harper said, "the point is that we can't approach this in any kind of conventional way. How we got control was purely through chance and observation, not logic. What we expected to happen today absolutely did not happen. Why not try something that seems ridiculous and unexpected?"

"Putting me back in charge would be unexpected," Krista's mother said.

"Oh my God," Krista said, "did you just make a joke?" Her mother just shrugged.

"Harper," James said, "please just tell us what you have in mind."

"What if there's a brief threat that's thwarted by an unlikely hero, reminding us to be thankful for the sense of safety we have and also creating an unlikely hero or two for everyone to love?"

Krista's mother rolled her eyes. "You want to be a popular hero, admired by all of your classmates."

"Not me," Harper said. "Steven Richards."

"And Tommy," James said, looking only at Krista's mother. The other two looked at him for a moment, then at each other, then back at Krista's mother. They didn't need to say a thing to each other.

"Yes," Harper said, "Instead of enhancing his rage and anxiety, use his determination and his drive to make him save everyone."

Krista's mother just stared at them for a moment, then she laughed; long and loud. "You think I'm the thing that's set him off? That he'd be just fine on his own?"

After a bit of quiet, Harper said, "You weren't influencing him at all?"

"Not as much as you seem to think. Good luck. When the threat comes, I'll push them in the right direction. Just let me know when it's coming and what it is."

Harper was looking at the table instead of Krista's mother. "Tomorrow," she said. "And you'll know. We'll let you loose right before it happens"

Krista's mother's smile faded. "All right," she said. "I'll be watching, and I'll cooperate."

James nodded and extended a hand. When Krista's mother raised an eyebrow, James said, "Shake on it."

Krista's mother slowly extended her own hand, looking uncertain. As they shook hands, she said, "I'll leave this woman for tonight, as part of our truce."

"Not quite yet," Krista said. She turned to Harper and James. "Guys," she said, "I know how to handle it, and, for some reason, I trust this thing anyway. But I want to ask some questions while I have some access to my mom without the usual crap and barriers."

James frowned. "But isn't there other crap and barriers?"

"Trust me, James," she said. "Call your parents and let me talk to my mother." She hugged James, then Harper, then she got up and touched her mother's shoulder. "Let's go in your room."

"How touching," Krista's mother said. "Let's bond."

~ * ~

When the three of them made it to school the next morning, their main interactions were smiling or nodding rather than speaking. They went about their day without directly discussing what would happen. It went on that way until lunch. When they were all at the table, James looked around the lunch hall and then asked, "Now?"

Harper narrowed her eyes a bit, then said, "Yes. Now."

Krista slowly slipped beneath the table. James closed his eyes and turned off all of the disrupters. At first, there wasn't much change. The students and monitors were still kind of loud and kind of moping around. Then, the lunch hall quieted down, but not in a calm way. It was more like the quiet when everybody stops talking to watch a fight that's about to break out. But none of them could have known how close to right they were.

Harper looked over to James. He still had his eyes closed, and his head was bowed. Harper looked from him to the hallway. She felt Krista (now invisible) brush past her leg. It was nearly a minute before the figure appeared in the lunch hall. It was covered head to toe in dark clothing, even with sunglasses and gloves. It was also carrying an axe. Not a gun, just an axe, though that certainly was concerning enough. James moaned just a little. To anyone else, it would probably just have seemed like he was concerned, but for Harper, it was clear that James was already starting to feel the strain. She looked back at the figure, then at Steven Richards.

Would the thing running the school be able to recognize who the figure was? Would they be able to coax Steven and Tommy into action as she said she would? While the rest of the lunch hall was turning and getting creeped out by the figure with the axe, Harper was feeling a whole different set of worries.

Things started to move very quickly from there. The figure shuffled in, dragging the axe as it went. Hopefully, the shock of seeing it and the return of the thing running the school would kickstart things. The figure headed to Tommy, the newly disabled and newly returned student that everyone had been crying over just the previous day. Harper was worried that one of the football players might try to be a hero, but the entity seemed to be good to its word, keeping them in check. Or maybe the football players were just actually scared. Whatever it was, they weren't the first to move. Steven stood up and ran at the figure from the side. He punched at it hard, and, for a second, Harper was afraid that James didn't have full shield up and Steven was really hurting Krista. If she was protected, then Krista did a good job of selling it.

Harper looked to James, but he was oblivious to her. His eyes were closed, and tears were forming at the edges. The figure stood and pushed away from Steven, leaving its back exposed to Tommy. Sure enough, Tommy pulled back and punched right at the lower back at the figure. It crumpled for a moment, then stood again. By this point, everyone in the lunch hall was screaming. The figure shuffled out, continually being pelted by food and silverware (the day's lunch was chicken nuggets and mashed potatoes with gravy, so it was an even mix of well-aimed, tiny projectiles and sloppy splats). Harper found herself smiling.

After the figure got away, Harper looked over at James. His head was almost all the way on the table, and he was drenched with sweat. Harper touched his hand. "Don't worry" she said quietly, "You can stop. I think that Krista is okay."

James let his head drop all the way to the table, and he let out a sigh. "I hope so," he said. One of the cool kids had gotten up and gone to Steven and Tommy, seeing if they were okay. After a few seconds, there was a huge cheer. Steven looked around like he was confused, but when Harper listened in, she could tell that they were happy. Really happy. Tommy too.

~ * ~

The performance had had the desired effect, and by the end of the day it was clear that the thing running the school was actually cooperating. Everyone remembered that Steven and Tommy had done something wonderful, but they tended to remember it differently, so they would talk about it for a bit, then they'd end up discussing how great Steven and Tommy were. Krista had been able to put everything in a garbage bag that she'd left in the woods. They would be able to take it and dump it without anyone finding it. After school, Krista, Harper, and James met up near the front doors. "So," Harper said, "it looks like it worked."

"Hard to believe," Krista said. "Plus it hurt like hell."

"Sorry that I didn't help enough," James said, looking at the floor.

Krista smiled and gently touched James's elbow. "You did. And thank you."

"Well," James said, still looking at the floor, "I appreciate that thanks, but Harper's use of the past tense would seem to imply that the matter is fully resolved. That's hardly the case."

"Fair enough," Harper said, "but I feel the calm, didn't you?"

"Wait," Krista said, "does that mean we're being controlled?"

Harper closed her eyes for a moment. "No," she said. "We do feel some of the same calm as everyone else, but that's because we don't feel tension in the school. It's not that we're being forced to feel it."

"So," Krista said, "What's next?"

"Slow and steady," James said, "We do small things, but we do them regularly. And we keep an eye on things to make sure that it's working."

Krista looked like she was about to say something, but she was interrupted. It was Steven Richards, "Hey," he said, looking at Harper and Krista first, then briefly at James. "Today has been, like, the best."

"That's awesome, Steven," Harper said. "You deserve a good day."

Steven nodded. It was hard to say how he took that. "Yeah," he said. "I mean, I guess everybody does, but I get it." He looked again at James and then Krista. "Hey," he said. "I really appreciate what you did for me."

"What do you mean?" Krista said.

Harper decided to try to read both Steven's words and his thoughts. It wasn't something that she ordinarily did. She was surprised when the two sounded like the same thing, like two people giving the same answer at almost the same time, "For reaching out. For believing in me. It worked."

"We're all so glad to hear it," James said. He shook Steven's hand. It was awkward but also kind of cute.

"All right," Steven said. "I'll see you around." With that he left.

When he was out of earshot, Krista said, "You listened to his thoughts, didn't you?"

Harper smirked, "Are you a mind reader, now?"

Krista shrugged, "I'm an astute observer of human behavior."

"Did you?" James asked.

"Yes," Harper said. "It was weird. It was like there was an echo."

"You think he was being controlled?" James asked.

"Or that it was the thing running the school talking right to us?" Krista asked.

Harper laughed. "I don't know. Maybe he just actually meant what he said and said what he was thinking."

"God," Krista said, "what a weirdo." the three of them laughed, not even so much at what Krista said as at whatever would give them a release.

"So," James said, "we believe that we're headed in a good direction?"

"We have to believe it," Harper said. "Or we might stop moving"

"Sure," James said, "but we should have a sense of when to redirect, when to change our approach and—"

"James," Krista said, "we will. I promise we'll make sure that we think about what we're doing. But for today, we need to rest and just go with the flow."

"Maybe we should propose 'the fighting canoes' as a new mascot," James said.

Krista laughed. She took James's hand and shook it. "James, don't ever change."

James nodded once and broke the shake. The three of them parted ways, all heading someplace different, but still all going home.

Acknowledgements

I would like to thank my family, my mother and father, my brother and his family, my wife, our daughter Cas and Nikki and Tina and Marcus. I would also like to thank Stephen Powers and Teresa Milbrodt for their support, thank you to Elyse, for your enthusiasm. Thank you to Aurora and Carmelo. Thanks to Erika, Prabhu, Kathy, Emily, Amanda, Chris, Joe, and Ann for being excellent colleagues. Thank you to Emily Lange for her hard work transcribing the first draft of this book from my very sloppy handwriting.

About the Author

Zeke Jarvis is a Professor of English at Eureka College. His work has appeared in *Cicada, Moon City Review*, and *KNOCK*, among other places. His books include *So Anyway...*, *In A Family Way, Lifelong Learning, Antisocial Norms* and *The Three of Them*.

**FOR THE FULL INVENTORY
OF QUALITY BOOKS**:
http://www.roguephoenixpress.com

Rogue Phoenix Press
Representing Excellence in Publishing

*Quality trade paperbacks and downloads
in multiple formats,
in genres ranging from historical to contemporary romance, mystery
and science fiction.
Visit the website then bookmark it.
We add new titles each month!*

www.ingramcontent.com/pod-product-compliance
Lightning Source LLC
Chambersburg PA
CBHW051958220626
47052CB00004B/991

9 781624 204890